THRESHOLD OF FIRE

A NOVEL OF FIFTH CENTURY ROME

HELLA S. HAASSE

*Translated by Anita Miller
and Nini Blinstrub*

Academy
Chicago
Publishers

Paperback edition published in 1996 by
Academy Chicago Publishers
363 West Erie Street
Chicago, IL 60610

The publisher gratefully acknowledges that publication
of the book was made possible in part by a grant from
the Foundation for the Production and Translation of
Dutch Literature

Printed and bound in the U.S.A. on acid-free paper.

Library of Congress Cataloging-in-Publication Data

Haasse, Hella S., 1918–
    [Nieuwer testament. English]
    Theshold of fire: a novel of fifth century Rome /
    Hella Haasse;
    translated by Anita Miller and Nini Blinstrub.
        p.   cm.
    ISBN 0-89733-390-X (hardcover)
    ISBN 0-89733-426-4 (paper)
    1. Rome — History — Empire, 30 B.C.–476 A.D.
    —Fiction. I. Title.
    PT5838.H45N513   1993
    839.3'1364—dc20   93-2465
                                           CIP

Qui fuerat genitor, natus nunc prosilit idem
Succeditque novus: geminae confinia vitae
Exiguo medius discrimine separat ignis.

Claudius Claudianus: *Phoenix*

CONTENTS

Introduction 9

I. The Prefect 19

II. Claudius Claudianus 113

III. The Prefect 207

Glossary 251

INTRODUCTION

In this dynamic novel, Hella Haasse illuminates a crucial, yet relatively obscure period of history — roughly 380 to 414 A.D., when Western civilization was undergoing a cataclysmic transformation from late antiquity to the early middle ages. The world was witnessing the death throes of the great Roman Empire — its unity destroyed by a cold war with Constantinople in the East, its military power evaporating before barbarian armies menacing its borders, and its cultural and religious heritage being stamped out by the Church Triumphant. The latter was an astonishing phenomenon: the total obliteration of a traditional religion, the destruction of a way of life.

Although Christianity was legalized in 312, it was under the Emperor Theodosius (346?-395) that it became the official religion of the Roman Empire. Theodosius was baptized in 380, the third year of his reign; he began the process which culminated in the liquidation of paganism and the repression

9

of heretics. Over fourteen years Theodosius issued a series of edicts: mandating faith in the Trinity, forbidding the use of altars and shrines for purposes of divination, shutting down pagan temples and eventually forbidding, on pain of death, sacrifices to man-made images. These policies were continued, more stringently, by Theodosius's inept son Honorius.

Theodosius had unquestionably helped to hasten the collapse of the Roman Empire by splitting it in two. On his death in 395, he divided it between Honorius and his elder and equally incompetent son Arcadius, who ruled the Eastern half from his capital in Constantinople. Honorius ruled the West, but it is another indication of impending disintegration that the Emperor no longer resided in Rome: it was too far from the threatened frontiers. He lived in Milan, a precedent that had been established by Constantine; but in 402 Gothic armies under Alaric besieged that city and nearly captured Honorius. So he moved the government to Ravenna, which was set in the midst of marshy tracts and water, and thus protected from invasion. Honorius, as we see in *Threshold of Fire*, rarely made "entry" into Rome.

Theodosius's sons have been called twilight men ruling in a twilight time. Both relied on regents: Honorius was guided by Flavius Stilicho, a respected Vandal general whose wife, Serena, was Theodosius's niece and adopted daughter. Arcadius was controlled first by Rufinus, a Gaul of bad reputation, and then by Eutropius, a eunuch who had been a slave. Great hostility developed between East and West. First Rufinus — who was torn to pieces by his own soldiers almost at the feet of Arcadius — and then Eutropius, were bitter enemies of Stilicho.

This is the background against which *Threshold of Fire* is set.

The action of the novel is circular, beginning and ending in July of 414 A.D. (although flashbacks extend its time span to about thirty-five years). We meet first the Prefect Hadrian, a Christian convert and transplanted Egyptian. We meet also Marcus Anicius Rufus, the only member of his devoutly Christian aristocratic family who has chosen to cling to the ancient Roman beliefs and practices. The Prefect heralds the frightening future; Marcus Anicius belongs to the dying past. Two other central figures in the novel are the Jew Eliezar ben

Elijah and the poet Claudius Claudianus.

Eliezar lives according to the tenets of his faith; he is, like Hadrian and Marcus Anicius, a dedicated man and, like them, a tormented one. He has a dark vision of things to come, although he is not for the moment in danger. He is left in peace by the authorities because Jews were assigned a unique place by Theodosius. In 393 their religion was recognized as legal, they were guaranteed right of assembly and their persons and property were officially protected from attack by Christians. But the handwriting was already on the wall: in 388 a synagogue was burned to the ground in Callinicum, a small town on the Persian border, by a fanatical mob led by the local bishop. Theodosius demanded restitution from the bishop on behalf of the Jewish population, but this demand was turned aside by Ambrose, Bishop of Milan, who prevented Theodosius from pursuing the matter.

Ambrose was a man of rigid principles who considered the fight against heresy to be a holy war, and who would give no quarter to Jews or pagans. His threats against Theodosius were the beginning of the subjection of temporal to spiritual power. The most striking example of this occurred when, on threat of excommunication, Ambrose forced Theodosius to do public penance for the massacre of seven thousand citizens at Thessalonica (now Salonica) in Greece.

It is around the character Claudius Claudianus, known to history as the poet Claudian, that the action flows. Claudian arrived in Italy apparently around 394 and a year or so later became poet to the court of Emperor Honorius. He is generally considered to be the last of the great Latin poets. He wrote panegyrics, invectives and epics, most of them celebrating the accomplishments of his hero and mentor Stilicho. He was a skilful propagandist, but far more than that. He was the master of Latin hexameter poetry under the Late Empire; his influence extended far beyond Italy into the Greek-speaking world. His work was carefully copied out by monks for over a thousand years, and has been invaluable to historians attempting to reconstruct the significant first decade of Honorius's reign: the tensions and political maneuverings, as well as the battles continually fought against rebels and barbarian chieftains who threatened the decaying sovereignity of Rome.

Claudian was heard from no more after 404.

This was not because he had lost favor with Stilicho, since Stilicho, before he was murdered in 408, arranged for an omnibus edition of Claudian's works. No one knows what happened to Claudian. It has been suggested that he died, or that he retired to Africa where Stilicho's wife Serena had arranged a marriage for him with a wealthy widow. But it has been suggested also that he got into trouble because of an epigram he wrote attacking the Prefect Hadrian, contrasting Hadrian's unsleeping rapacity with the indolent honesty of Mallius Theodorus, consul in 399, for whom Claudian wrote a panegyric, and whom he clearly liked and respected.

Claudian glorified Rome: he saw it as it had been and not as it was. And he saw it through non-Christian eyes. Except for a few ambiguous lines, there is no reference to Christianity in Claudian's poetry. And although he wrote on mythological themes, he did not necessarily accept the Roman pantheon. It is a reflection of the Prefect's fanaticism, and possible ignorance, that looking through the book-rolls in Marcus Anicius's library, he comments with disapproval on "verses teeming with mythological names"; this was the accepted practice in the poetry of the time, a convention, and not even the bishops complained about it. It should be noted, incidentally, that Marcus Anicius, looking to the past, uses book-rolls at a time when the codex, with its sewn binding, had largely replaced them, thanks to the emphasis placed by Christians upon the Scriptures.

Thus Claudius Claudianus, poet and humanist, stands apart from both the doomed pagan Marcus Anicius, who yearns for a Rome that is lost forever, and the tormented Christian Hadrian, who, like Bishop Ambrose, has spent his life in the Roman civil administration, which was known to breed narrow authoritarianism. Hadrian views the world as Ambrose does, with restricted vision; it is Ambrose and Hadrian who are the wave of the future. Theirs is the state of mind responsible eventually not only for the Inquisition, but for the untold suffering caused by uncompromising political movements in our own century.

Anita Miller
Chicago, Illinois
May, 1993

The novel falls into three parts. The first, "The Prefect", begins early in the morning on the fifth of July, 414; the second, "Claudius Claudianus", is set three weeks earlier and the action moves forward to the fourth of July; the third section, called "The Prefect" once again, takes place in the late afternoon and evening of the fifth of July and the morning of the sixth of July.

I.

THE PREFECT

1.

The leather curtain closes behind the soldiers. Uneasily, the prisoners survey the judgment hall and find it changed: hazy early morning light filters through the curved windows cut into the masonry between the columns. All of those who have been brought in are familiar with the Prefect's tribunal from the period before the Gothic invasion: some of them had appeared here as witnesses, others as accusers — one of them, ten years before, as the accused. At that time there had been a view, through the open gallery, of an inner court and the walls of the former temple of Tellus. Now nothing of the outside world is visible except the light coming through the high window recesses.

The only person in the room who does not look about, but keeps his eyes fixed on the floor at his feet — black and white meandering mosaics — can tell from the change in sounds — until then subdued as usual — that the Prefect has entered. A chair is being moved.

In the foreground of the Prefect's field of vision

(on occasions like this, the praetorians are nothing more to him than part of the furniture: self-evident, scarcely perceived) are six men, three of whom he knows personally; he will soon address them without hesitation by name and surname: he has expected them to be there, since their presence is the result of prolonged, meticulous maneuvering. He allows himself the luxury of ignoring them, of delaying the encounter with their impassive faces and cold eyes. Then — a long look at the other three.

None of them seems like a complete stranger to him. His eyes come to rest on the last man in the row, whose face is averted: a beard, a frayed toga — a strange bird among these patricians. Out of step with the others. But the Prefect has the feeling — for reasons he cannot immediately identify — that this person will play a crucial role in the proceedings. Quickly he searches his memory, scouring various strata of his official activities: a place, a time, an event? At this moment he knows that there is something more here than meets the eye — something that goes much deeper. His satisfaction at the arrest — finally! — of what he considers to be a subversive group, is no longer unclouded. There has been a subtle shift. This affair no longer holds the prospect of a careful savoring of victory, of pleasure at the demonstration of the power of authority. It has become hollow at the core.

He gestures toward his officials.

"Today, on the third day of Nones of July, in the fifth hour after sunset, I, Aulus Fronto, Commander of the third division of the praetorian guard, made, with my men, a raid on the dwelling of Marcus Anicius Rufus on Janiculus Hill. I found Marcus Anicius Rufus and his wife Sempronia in company with a few noblemen who upon request identified themselves to us: Marcellinus Maximus, Flaccus Vescularius, Gaius Agerius Flestus, Quintus Fulcinius Trio. They were being served by three slaves: Phoebus, Milo, Herman. Upon investigation, it developed that the rest of the staff had orders not to show themselves in that part of the villa after the third hour.

"When I entered the *tablinum*, the situation was as follows: the couches were pushed together so that they formed three sides of a square. Marcus Anicius Rufus, his wife Sempronia and their previously mentioned guests were lying with their backs to tables on which I saw the remains of a meal. In the space which had been formed were two persons, a man and a woman calling themselves Pylades and Urbanilla, mimes by profession, who were engaged — at the request of Marcus Anicius Rufus, according to their statements — in giving a performance of the love dance of the god Dionysus and his bride Ariadne, said performance being forbidden by decree of our august Emperor Honorius in the twelfth year of his reign.

"In the garden I discovered two more members of the artistic troupe: the weightlifter Balcho and Homullus, a dwarf, disguised as Priapus. A pagan altar was standing in readiness. Upon searching the house, I found, in one of the anterooms, some baskets of live cocks; there was also a case containing instruments and objects customarily used for sacrifice and the inspection of entrails. All three slaves had seen the baskets, but alleged that they did not know who put them there. The men who, on my orders, guarded the hilly terrain around the villa seized an individual hiding in the bushes: he calls himself Niliacus and has no fixed domicile.

"He denies having had any contact with Marcus Anicius Rufus and his household. When confronted with him, everyone present stated that they had never seen the man before; Marcus Anicius Rufus, however, said this only after long hesitation. The slave Milo, when we showed him the means of coercion last night in the prison, declared that the person named Niliacus had been in the villa once before, and that was on the day of the triumphant entry of our august Emperor Honorius, three weeks ago around the hour of sunset.

"Letters, books and other documents from the library of Marcus Anicius Rufus were confiscated by me and delivered under seal to the office of the Prefect."

With the exception of Marcus Anicius Rufus, all the prisoners have been taken back to the holding rooms. The interrogation can begin.

The Prefect does not speak immediately. Nor does he look at the accused, but contemplates his own right hand, spread flat against the arm of his chair. He raises one shoulder slightly; the folds of his mantle fall from his outstretched arm. His right foot, in its red shoe, is thrust far forward, reaching almost to the edge of the platform. Because of these arrests, he was awakened earlier than usual, before sunrise. He had been impatiently awaiting the news that

Marcus Anicius Rufus and his friends had been brought to the prefecture for immediate trial, but even this welcome information could not erase the memory of his strange, early morning dream . . .

He had found himself on a barren, desolate coast. A rocky precipice, without a trace of vegetation, descended perpendicularly to a narrow gravel beach. The sun did not shine, the sea was grey. The enclosed bay was shaped like a half-moon and deserted, despite signs of human presence: the rocks had been fashioned to resemble the façade of a temple; a row of pillars, cut out of the stone, supported a triangular frieze crowded with vague figures — perhaps nothing but rock formations. Wide steps, crumbling in many places, descended to the sea. Between the columns stood disfigured sculpture, the most striking a relief representing a right hand, raised in oath. While he stood there in his dream, he thought he heard someone call his name. . .

As he dressed, he decided that it must have been his secretary's voice that he had heard.

"Marcus Anicius Rufus, you are accused of having

organized a gathering in your house for the secret practice of magic, the intention being the destruction of our august Emperor and the ruination of the Empire. Do you admit these facts?"

"I invited a few friends to dinner and to an artistic performance. I don't see anything unusual about that — much less incriminating."

"This performance had the character of a pagan ritual. The dancers were at the point of committing the act of love in public."

"The company was portraying the myth of Bacchus and Ariadne. I had requested an artistic performance — not erotic scenes, which I would never have tolerated."

"The dwarf's attire left nothing to the imagination."

"I didn't see the dwarf in that costume. The artists got dressed while we were dining. All I knew was that they were going to perform a number from the classical mime-repertoire. At the moment when the centurion and his men burst into my house — a breach of domestic peace against which I wish to register a strong protest — it's true that the dancers were miming an embrace. But everyone present, and primarily the artists themselves, can testify that there was no question that it was simply a pretence."

"Actors are not heard as witnesses, you should know that. The Commandant, Aulus Fronto, has the right to enter any place where he suspects trouble. He and his men are unanimous in their declaration that the dancers' position could be open to only one interpretation."

"The entry of the praetorian guards caused some confusion. At the moment none of us was looking at the artists. In my opinion the impressions of the commander and his men are based on some sort of optical illusion . . ."

"But you *do* admit that you ordered a performance of the love dance of the pagan gods Bacchus and Ariadne? That's enough . . . "

"Once more, it should be obvious that I'm relying here on time-honored cultural traditions —"

"Those Roman citizens who are aware of their responsibilites know that nowadays they must indulge in other entertainments at home. The report says further that in one of your anterooms, my officers found baskets of live cocks, undoubtedly sacrificial animals . . . "

"No orders were given for sacrifice in my house. I don't know who brought them in or who received them —"

"There were often sacrifices in your house. Fresh flowers were placed on your house altar and at the feet of idols."

"Animal sacrifice has never taken place under my roof and it never will take place there!"

"Ah, that's a clever play on words! In your garden — in the open air and thus, I grant you, not under your roof — was a small altar, the kind that can be set up and taken down quickly."

"I don't know anything about that. It was dark in the garden. I didn't think it was necessary to examine the actors' stage properties beforehand."

"In the jurisprudence of actions connected with magic, innumerable examples are cited of rituals identical to those which were apparently going to take place in your house last night: an erotic performance culminating in the sacrifice of cocks, including the so-called inspection of entrails. And all this in order to obtain an answer to questions about the duration of the Emperor's life and to exercise an influence on that duration — in short, a detestable preamble to high treason. It's an undisputed fact that the materials necessary for these kinds of practices have been found in your house, ready for use."

"Yes, well, despite all that, I suggest you need only question the artists — unofficially if necessary. Since they are outside society, not legally responsible citizens, they just might know more than you or I — "

"Your sarcasm is misplaced. I have informed myself to the last minute detail. For a number of understandable reasons, actors never carry with them instruments associated with such actions — they're intimidated by the law, and they're afraid of reprisals from those who make their living from sacrifice and divination."

"I can assure you that no one who was in my house last night considers himself qualified to perform those rituals that you're talking about."

"You haven't really explained the presence of the man called Niliacus."

"I repeat what I said earlier: his presence on my property last night was unknown to me. I don't know what he was doing there."

"May I help you remember? Was he perhaps waiting for some prearranged signal? You had met him before, you know."

"I refuse to discuss the allegations made by a slave frightened of torture."

"If you answer truthfully, you'll spare the slave real pain and save yourself the trouble of inventing explanations for what you won't be able to deny in the long run."

"Since you are determined to find me guilty, why don't you just tell me right now what it is you wish to hear?"

"Did you summon this man Niliacus — whose name, origin and circumstances are so strikingly nebulous — to sacrifice cocks and make certain prophecies during the gathering at your home?"

"No, I did nothing of the sort."

"Marcus Anicius Rufus, you — in unfortunate contrast to the rest of your respected family, past and present — are not a Christian. We know you to be a man who holds stubbornly to pagan practices, to an obsolete mode of life . . . You refuse to admit that times have changed. We remember your words and actions at critical moments in the Senate. You've never been able to hide your displeasure with recent developments — worse, you have revealed a deep-rooted antipathy to the views of the exalted Emperor Honorius and his advisors. There are persistent rumors that you have publicly urged the restoration of ancient values. In addition, there is no doubt about the inclinations of your guests. Denial is pointless. I have reliable information. This wouldn't be the first time that a *coup d'etat* was prepared under the guise of a dinner among friends — with criminal sacrifice and prophesying camouflaged as the buffoonery of supposed artists."

"You have no proof of that."

"In my opinion, both the nature and the intention of the performance in your house are indisputable."

"Then I must demand legal assistance."

"Considering the incriminating character of the facts and the seriousness of the transgression, that's absolutely unnecessary."

"It's only your interpretation of the facts that makes them incriminating. You and your officers have blown this affair completely out of proportion. All that really happened is that I invited the mime Pylades — I enjoyed his performances in the past — to come and amuse my guests with one of the numbers that were popular in his heyday. Before dessert — following ancient custom — I had the statues of my ancestors and my household gods set upon a table and I poured wine to honor them. Now that's called idolatry, it's punishable, I know that. I'm ready to pay any penalty that you decide to impose. I swear on oath that this is all there is. Now let's have an end to this undignified spectacle."

"We're going around in circles, Marcus Anicius Rufus. You can't deny the presence in your house of compromising persons and objects and you have given me no satisfactory explanation for that. This is a serious matter. You're under suspicion of high treason."

"In other words, you want to ruin me and my friends. Now I understand why the commander of the guard thought he had the right to force his way into my house. That raid was premeditated."

"I'm only an instrument of justice. I feel personally concerned about what is happening to you and your friends today. It would grieve me to have to remove you from office, to see you deprived of power and wealth. Nevertheless, I feel no pity for you. Some must fall very low before they're able to find the truth. You have always closed your eyes and ears to the new; you have always been arrogantly opposed to the spirit of our times. You are literally *outside* our time, Marcus Anicius Rufus – that's proven by your desire to use incantation and bloody sacrifice to control the future, to meddle in things that belong only to God. I hope fervently that what happened today will bring you insight, help you to regain humility and show you the way to true salvation."

"All right, punish me then if you have to, but I beg you to leave my family and my friends alone."

"I can't leave anyone alone who was discovered on your premises last night. My heart is bleeding, but I must enforce the law."

"Enforce it then, but don't insult my intelligence with these elaborate speeches —"

"I wonder if you would be able to maintain this stoical attitude under all circumstances . . . ?"

"I've said what I had to say. Nothing in the world could make me say anything else. And I know my friends — it's the same for them."

"This man, this Niliacus. . . clearly *he* doesn't belong to your distinguished circle of friends. Perhaps *he* will prove . . . willing — or should I say, more sensitive to certain methods of persuasion . . . if that should become necessary . . . "

"He's a complete outsider."

"I can't accept that, as long as I don't know the reason for your involvement with him."

"It's a private matter of no importance."

"I have the impression that you have a strong reason to protect him."

"I came upon the man by accident in the street — he looked like someone I knew once. After I had invited him to visit my home, I discovered my mistake."

"And when was that?"

"My slave told you — on the day of the entry of the Emperor Honorius, three weeks ago."

"And who was it you thought he resembled?"

"That's certainly beside the point — it has nothing to do with the situation."

"Nevertheless, I find it extremely interesting."

"I'm not standing before a nosy old woman, am I — but before the first magistrate in the City —"

"Your insults can only make matters worse. Stop and think about your charming wife Sempronia whom I must still interrogate . . . You still refuse to answer? Niliacus will certainly tell me everything soon."

"All I know is that you won't get to hear what you insist on hearing. Since I am not allowed to defend myself fairly and you've obviously made up your mind to destroy me, all discussion between us is meaningless. From this moment, I will not say another word to you."

The statements of the four others, the guests of

Marcus Anicius Rufus, are identical. They come one after the other, to stand before the Prefect; all — depending on their temperaments and the extent of their self-command — grimly stiff or convincingly indifferent, unshaven, the traces of a sleepless night on their faces, but with their togas correctly draped over arm and shoulder. Just as their host had done, all four ask for lawyers. Four times the Prefect refuses, pointing out that as the representative of the highest authority in the City, he is fully qualified — yes, required — to pronounce judgment in cases like these, behind closed doors, without jury, without counsel, without defense, and within twenty-four hours.

It had not been his secretary's voice that he had heard. His name had been called, a faint, distant, drawn-out sound: Hadrian! A cry from the sea, against the wind. He was standing then on the bottom step of the broad staircase, with every wave a thin, shiny film washing over the granite. In his dream, he saw the myriad pebbles of the sloping shore moving under the water. Slivers in the mosaic on the floor before his platform gleam like wet stones. The sun is higher in the sky; there are fewer shadows in the corners of the justice hall. Some sounds are still coming from the doorway through which Quintus Fulcinius Trio has just been led away: footsteps ring in the hollow corridor beyond it. The low voices of the praetorian guard summon the next prisoner for interrogation; their weapons and greaves clink softly against the metal-covered leather scallops of their breastplates.

The Prefect's officials, arrayed in a semi-circle behind him, whisper together. He can hear the rustle of their garments and the shuffling of their feet as they move about. Someone stifles a cough. He knows that he need only tap his signet ring against the arm of his chair to obtain complete silence, which he values above all else during a session — the wall of living statues behind him underlining the atmosphere of impassive, dignified expectancy which befits his role as deputy to His Majesty. But that he makes no attempt to call his retinue to order, by tapping with the onyx on the index finger of his left hand, is more evidence of the uncertainty which came over him when he saw the prisoners standing before him. He feels thwarted, in some inexplicable fashion checkmated, unjustly deprived of satisfaction, injured in the most essential part of himself: the belief in his duty. Is this the after-effect of a dream?

Behind the impressive façade with the columns, an impenetrable precipice, and before him as far as the eye can reach, the equally impenetrable sea.

"Hadrian!"

It did not seem to be a summons, nor a greeting. The sound grew fainter, more protracted and melancholy, and there on the most extreme edge of that place without depth, without landscape, he had, on the threshold between sleep and waking, realized in dismay the profundity of his loneliness.

"Niliacus? Nothing more? No last name, no first name? A foreigner?"

"Born on the Nile as the name tells you, but I've been in Rome for a long time."

"So you're not a Roman citizen?"

"No more nor no less than you yourself."

The Prefect's studied impassivity stiffens under the pressure of a sudden instinctive defensiveness; this creates a still deeper silence around him, as if everyone is holding his breath. Who can be more Roman than the City's highest magistrate sitting in judgment on the dais, his sallow skin stretched, shining as if it were polished, over forehead, cheekbones and chin, eyes just as dark and opaque as the seal on his finger, accentuated by the immaculate folds which flow from shoulders to toes, horizontal and vertical, pleats and creases, blue white against cream white – the only broken line is the purple band bordering his garments, which seems to be drawn in blood.

For the first time in many years, feelings stir in the Prefect which he thought had been dispelled; they smart like old wounds. He suspects that all the officials behind him have been reminded now of what they have always known: that Hadrian, born and raised in Alexandria, in Egypt, is an imported Roman – yes, he too is a Niliacus – and that this knowledge, despite the respect shown him (his due) could once again (as in earlier days) rouse in his inferiors an intolerable tendency to behave toward him with condescending familiarity. This thought alienates him from the self-image which he has cultivated for so long: his outward appearance, his bearing and the ceremonial toga, seem a brittle shell within which he cringes, vulnerable.

Reason is powerless here. The word "Egypt" – which has been in everyone's thoughts, but which no one has yet uttered – possesses, perhaps even before it is grasped by the mind, the force of an exorcism. Pharos, the lighthouse at Alexandria, a white needle in the morning light, a forefinger raised against the sky before us as, from the afterdeck of a ship on its way to Rome, we saw the familiar coastline fade away forever . . . .

In his dream, the little ship sailed without him. He was called by name, his Roman name: Hadrian! But he must remain behind, an exile in a land only one arcade deep, unreal as the backdrop of a theatre. Marble steps rise to the quays of Alexandria, they rise out of the sea to the colonnades of the buildings. The desolate region of his dreams — was it an hermetically sealed country of origin, an Egypt become inaccessible? How can one tell what is hiding behind there, or lying fossilized in the rocks?

The interrogation continues. More cautiously now, with mounting suspicion — and another feeling, too: a disturbing tension. The Prefect gropes for information about this man in the shabby cloak. A freedman, yes, practicing no craft, no, lives from hand to mouth. No, he had nothing to do with the events in the villa of Marcus Anicius Rufus.

"But you had been in that house once before.

Marcus Anicius Rufus has admitted it."

A shrug, a longer pause than after the first questions.

"What do you want to know?"

"The reason for your first visit."

"I didn't visit Marcus Anicius Rufus."

"Ah, yes, then it was he who approached you. What did he want with you?"

"A while ago I was attacked during a fight in the street —"

"On the day of the entry of the exalted Emperor Honorius?"

"That's right. Marcus Anicius Rufus saw this in passing and saved me by taking me home with him in his retinue."

"No one acts like that toward a total stranger."

"Possibly he mistook me for someone else. I thanked him and left again. That's all."

"Whom did he take you for then?"

"I didn't ask him that."

"What were you doing near his house last night?"

"I was looking for a place to sleep. Since the Emperor's entry, there are many people in the City. When I was leaving Marcus Anicius Rufus's house that time, I saw how peaceful the garden was and filled with jasmine —"

The Prefect is irritated by this air of indifference bordering on impertinence, from one who belongs without question to the most destitute social caste.

"That's enough! The City and the provinces are swarming with charlatans disguised as vagabonds who privately perpetuate their pagan hocus pocus for money. Their equipment includes portable altars and cases with sacrificial knives. The praetorian guard have frequently confiscated items like these. Unfortunately, too many of our highly placed citizens, who should know better, are secretly greedy for prophecies and black arts — if not for something still worse. It is curious that you were so close to the villa where, as has been proven, preparations had been made for the sacrifice of cocks. Everything that has come to light during these hearings has confirmed my belief that the mealtime at Marcus Anicius Rufus's was far from being as innocent as some would like us to think. Both Marcus Anicius Rufus and you must provide me with more credible explanations before I feel I have reason to revise my opinion. Prove to me first of all that Marcus Anicius did not send for you on the recommendation of like-minded friends, that you have never sacrificed a cock . . ."

The man facing the Prefect moves a step nearer on the meandering mosaics and raises his right hand.

"I can't prove anything. Besides, it's the accuser who must supply the proof. But I swear that I have never sacrificed a cock unless it was in your presence."

Later — the hearing is suspended until further notice — in an adjoining room where the confiscated books and personal property of Marcus Anicius Rufus are displayed, the Prefect absorbs the full significance of that last remark. As he takes up the rolls of parchment, glances at the wax tablets (the clerks, busy since midnight reading line by line, declare that so far they have found no incriminating material), the words of Niliacus, born on the Nile, hang in the air, a disturbing echo. Why that gnawing feeling of dissatisfaction, even of secret fear? That question is closely connected to another which the Prefect must admit to his consciousness: why, when surprise and displeasure were clearly written on the faces of his officials, did he not go on to interrogate the enigmatic foreigner? To elicit personal details — from which village, which city on the Nile have you come, what brought you to Rome, when and how, who gave you your freedom?

Indistinct images of the past flash before him, startling because they make the Prefect realize that his past — Egypt, his youth — form a backdrop made of basalt which cannot be destroyed. The mud huts of the Fayyum, lotus blossoms floating on the brown reflecting water of the Nile inlets in the swampy Delta, the long rows of lighted pleasure boats moored outside Canopis, the suburb of Alexandria . . . . his father's house . . . the fragrance of forgotten meals . . . the sounds of the vernacular which he has not spoken since he was a little child. For more than thirty years, he has been a Roman. Magistrate of the Empire, a vocation for a bachelor who has left all his relatives behind in Egypt, who has no circle of friends and no inclination to indulge in forms of amusement which require intimacy with others. . . He has dedicated himself completely to the task set him by two emperors in succession.

Because of the painstaking performance of his duty, the fastidious observance of even the slightest detail of procedure, he has become more and more convinced that he has earned the right to his second birth as a Roman citizen. Egyptians are considered to be capricious, to be oriented toward Greece, filled with an old resentment of a triumphant Rome. Hadrian, honorary Roman, more Roman than the Romans, presumes distrust when there is no reason for it at all; is ashamed — worse, sometimes offended — even when Egypt is mentioned innocently. He does not wish to analyze his reactions; he has chosen to turn his back on the petrifying past; he has tried by drastic methods to free himself from those bonds. For ten years he believed he had banned thoughts of that rupture, painful as a wound . . . .

But a dream, a sudden encounter with a certain Niliacus (whose last remark seems to have separated them from the others and joined them together) have shrivelled away two decades of Roman grand style. The hand of the other, this Niliacus, raised in an oath . . .

"I swear that I have never sacrificed a cock unless it was in your presence."

That piece of stone in the dream, that relief, a raised hand: "I swear. . ." But what, when, how? Dreams, it is said, are a mixture of memory and premonition . . . Is it a residue of paganism to think like this, to attach so much importance to a dream? Hadrian has never seen a cock sacrificed.

Never?

Before him on the table are rows of boxes holding rolls of books. The clerks stand waiting for the inspection to end. Once again, the Prefect unrolls one of the volumes. Again, as so often, he is overcome by the need to demonstrate his authority and expert knowledge – all the more after the slight drop in attitude and appearance which no one in the justice hall could have missed. Beautiful letters, regular and even on the page – Marcus Anicius Rufus had capable calligraphers among his slaves. Verses teeming with mythological names. . . this choice of reading matter only confirms what the Prefect already knows. A shameful devotion to the pagan legacy!

Hadrian presses his lips together in disapproval, restraining the testy impulse to roll the paper up again. He recognizes the metaphor, the style: the epigram that he holds before him is inscribed word-for-word in his memory. The blood drains from his face.

> While Mallius dreams in daylight
> and darkness
> The Egyptian steals everything; nothing
> is sacred to him.

People of Rome, cry with one voice:
Mallius, wake!
Perhaps then the light of Egypt will fade away.

Ten years ago, in these same rooms, there had been another interrogation. The accused at that time was the poet whose work, adeptly copied by Marcus Anicius Rufus's slave-scribe, now lies exposed on the desk of the prefecture; the writer of that epigram which passed from mouth to mouth, received with scornful laughter and malicious enjoyment. Don't these walls hold an echo? Aren't the coldest phrases charged with passion, and doesn't that passion remain even after the words themselves have died away forever? *Then* — ten years ago — Hadrian had scarcely been able to control the trembling of his hands during that interrogation, that game of question-and-answer . . . A game indeed — that was more than ever a comedy of justice performed in an orderly way to give an appearance of objectivity to what was really an act of personal vengeance.

In the place reserved for the accused, the young man, the court poet fallen into disfavor, looked him straight in the eye, his lip curled in contempt; he did not yet believe in the seriousness of this procedure: he was undoubtedly thinking of his powerful friends

— or of those among the powerful whom he took to be his friends — and most of all of his constant benefactor Flavius Stilicho, the guardian, father-in-law and advisor of Emperor Honorius and virtual ruler of the Occidental Empire. The Prefect, however, his palms wet with emotion, knew that this accused's hopes for help were futile, that the nature of the indictment, the risk of scandal at that exact moment, would render Flavius Stilicho powerless.

Oh, how intolerable that black haughty look in a face darker in complexion than is usual among the Roman elite — but how comforting his own certainty of seeing that calm expression wiped away, of seeing this illustrious protégé of the great kicked off his pedestal, how soothing to watch doubt and helplessness creep over that self-confident mask.

"Name?"

"Claudius Claudianus."

"Position?"

"Notary tribune, court poet."

"Accused of the practice of magic, of sacrificing to idols. Suspected of abusive practices. . . ."

No one in the justice hall betrayed by look or gesture that he knew what all Rome knew: that the Prefect of the City, Hadrian, was standing eye-to-eye with a former client and longtime intimate friend who had turned into a hated enemy; that the Prefect had seized the opportunity now to destroy the man whom, a few years earlier, he had not dared accuse of defamation for fear of making himself ridiculous. Four lines of verse which had been on everyone's lips about the "Egyptian" and his avarice — these were undoubtedly in the thoughts of more than one of those attending the proceedings. This realization certainly helped the Prefect to overcome his feelings of uncertainty. Vigilance — yes, like the Pharos lighthouse, the light of Egypt, he would show himself to be pitilessly vigilant, an example to anyone who might think that the authority of the Empire, as it is vested in those who represent it, could be mocked with impunity.

Claudius Claudianus — eliminated, excluded forever from the world of the living. Every trace of him removed. Or is that an illusion? The epigram has lost none of its corrosive force. Four lines, written many years ago, brought to light again by accident in the private library of one accused in a later trial, possesses the power to summon back a vanished man, to reopen an old wound.

"We don't need this here," the Prefect says. He

pushes the book roll ("The Works of Claudianus") away from him across the table top. "It has no connection with the matters under discussion to-day."

But as he leaves the anteroom, he feels that he has been the victim of an illusion. His eyes and ears perceive signs of a presence which he refuses to acknowledge; his instinct tells him more than his intellect. In an instant he will have crossed a threshold — not just the tangible threshold of the justice hall. A voice behind him (one of the police officials) asks whether the instruments should be prepared for the more stringent interrogation. With a hasty wave of his hand, Hadrian delegates the decision.

A ghost has been called up in the silent justice hall — the poet who was condemned ten years earlier. He clings to the Prefect as though he were his shadow. The sun comes through the window niches now so that the Prefect cannot move or turn without seeing, at his feet or next to him or opposite him on the wall, the dull blot of his own opacity.

He always thinks of Claudius Claudianus as a dead man, because the verdict he had pronounced upon him (exclusion from water and fire and thus hunger, thirst and homelessness; complete isolation from people inside a circumference of one hundred miles with the City in the center) was in fact a death sentence. An unwritten law, applied since the time of the Twelve Tables, holds that one thrust out in this way can be stabbed with impunity as soon as he sets foot in the forbidden territory. At the time, the Prefect had taken certain steps, given certain commands. There is a blind spot in his memory. Had no one told him the outcome or had he intentionally ignored the report? He has to acknowledge that after ten years he doesn't really know whether Claudius Claudianus is still alive.

What ghosts have appeared in the wake of Marcus Anicius Rufus and his clique of patrician pagans? Even if there has been no actual sacrifice in the villa, it is nevertheless true that they all believe in the power of magic. Their idolatry is a form of exorcism. They commit their crimes brazenly wherever there is darkness, evil . . . all the horrors and troubling secrets of a dead sinful world arise once more through the breaches they create, to threaten the peace of the soul, achieved at so high a price. Pious hermits in the mountains of Umbria have told Hadrian how, with their own eyes, they had seen pitch-black demons crawling out of a hole in the ground toward a secret offering which still smoldered on a pagan altar. Through persistent pagan practices, Marcus Anicius Rufus and his friends appear to have eclipsed the light of the sun and to have caused one word to buzz in the Prefect's brain like a poisonous insect: the Nile, the Nile.

2.

An image rises from the depths of time. Clearly standing out from hordes of memories, an estate in the Nile Delta. It belongs to one Eliezar ben Ezekiel, one of the richest men in Alexandria. A walled villa and outbuildings, a small settlement set among fields, olive groves, fishponds. Eliezar, who has just come from the city, is receiving a high official in the service of Rome, the young Hadrian, who has only recently been appointed. The entertainment includes a circular cruise among the reeds.

Memory focuses on a flimsy lean-to of woven reeds standing on one of the countless marshy islands; a raft, tied to poles thrust in the mud. A boat, a dahabyeh manned by oarsmen, has just come along the narrow canals between the reeds. Under the striped awning, host and guest are seated. Both Eliezar's hands are raised in anger and dismay . . . why? Statues move, come to life: half-naked youths, surprised in their hiding place, leap away from a fire-blackened stone used since time immemorial by the farm workers for secret sacrifices to the ancient

fertility gods. One of the youths — still only a child
— turns toward the landowner in the boat and, in a
gesture that is at once defiant and defensive, shows
the palms of his hands, smeared with the blood of
the cock lying at his feet.

Now, more than twenty-five years later, in the
prefecture of Rome, all the impressions and feelings
of that moment revive in the memories of two men
for whom the words "born on the banks of the Nile"
are key. Close, sultry heat, the stink of mud, the cries
of the ibis flying above the endless masses of rustling
reeds . . . For Hadrian, the Prefect, the unforgettable
sensation of the boat rocking in flashing water; for
the other, the man held under suspicion in the
holding room, purely sensual impressions — the
prickling of sharp corn-stubble under his feet — are
as strong as ever, but the thoughts and feelings of
that moment have faded long ago, replaced by new
interpretations.

The incident itself — some youths caught by Eliezar and his guest in the act of sacrificing, or playing
at sacrificing, to gods, against the landowner's express prohibition — that is the surface action, the
simple direct beginning of an affair which has grown
most complicated over the years, branching out in

many directions until the day of the trial of Marcus
Anicius Rufus.

Those things which are most hidden — the desire
or the aversion of one individual, even those im-
pulses which are never completely conscious — can
turn the scale, determine the lives and destinies of
others, call up actions and reactions which, years
later, that man cannot control.

Let us take the case of Eliezar ben Ezekiel who, in
the zenith of his manhood, has reached that stage of
life when one becomes aware that old age is approaching. An experienced man who understands
people, who has earned his insights through sorrow
and bitterness; a pious man whose passion for justice
makes him incapable of charity . . .

On the evening of the discovery in the canefields
— first of all, he had sent the boys home, then
courteously bade his guest Hadrian farewell — he is
now alone in the room draped with mosquito
netting and lit by the glimmer of an oil lamp, where
he sleeps when he is staying at the villa. Seven steps
forward, seven steps back — his caftan trails behind
him over the floor . . . frowning, talking softly but
vehememtly to himself, his right hand squeezed into

a fist before his heart, or turned palm upward, fingers spread, in a gesture of prayer, or even supplication . . . Now and then, he pauses at a table set with an ongoing game of chess; he takes up a piece, moves it, shoves it back. The night wind rises, stirs the gauze curtains. Someone is playing a flute in one of the outbuildings. There is a marshy odor in the air; it smells of the Nile. There is no one to witness Eliezar's restlessness and confusion. The boy who cut the cock's throat is his own son's son.

When the mother — an Egyptian slave — died of fever, Eliezar placed the small child with the family of an overseer on the estate. His nicknames — "Little One", "Sonny", "Hey You" — were quickly out-grown. The names passed on from father to son are Ezekiel, Nathan, Mordecai — one of these is what the family heir should be called, but his son's son has no place in his family. So he allows the boy to be called by a name similar to his Egyptian mother's name — Klafthi. The people of the estate know nothing, the child is considered an orphan, a foundling, taken under the wing of the generous landlord. Eliezar's son — he has married during this time and is the father of daughters only — never comes here from Alexandria; he is involved in other business and has no interest in the land.

A child's game — imitating a half-understood primitive ritual like those practiced by the fellahs outside the enclosures of the estate, cock's blood washed away in the twinkling of an eye and forgotten — one can look at these things objectively, without attaching too much importance to them. If anyone else were involved, Eliezar would silently repress his disgust and then take steps to prevent that sort of thing from happening again. But the look of that boy — his whole body tense with the shock of being caught, the tendon trembling in his outstretched foot — this struck Eliezar with the force of a blow. Nathan, Mordecai, Ezekiel . . . but there is something unformed, wild, hidden there . . . the still unborn grandson close by and yet unreachable in the shape of a slave child, no different at first glance from the countless others who wander about the grounds.

In one single second, the look in those eyes, glimpsed across the narrow strip of water between the boat and the island, betrayed an infallible instinct mixed with an even more definite will to resist. It was that expression, above two bloody hands, which caused Eliezar to raise his own hands to heaven in pain, anger, shame — as when a beloved child behaves in a stupid, scandalous way. But he quickly stifled this reaction: he wished to appear, in the eyes of Hadrian, the representative of Rome, to be merely the landlord who ordered the boys, with restrained severity, to return home immediately on the raft in the wake of his boat and who instructed his servants to purify the spot in the canefields by burning it down before sunset. The young magistrate felt compelled, with the fervor of the recent convert to Christianity, to voice both his abhorrence at pagan custom and his familiarity with it, in the same breath. Eliezar found his pedantry almost unbearably irritating.

He brings the oil lamp to the recess where his bed stands, but he cannot sleep. The guilt of his son, who created this child out of unthinking lust, and created with him a whole world of acts and thoughts — that guilt is *his* guilt too. Where and how did he fail to instill respect for the Law and the Commandments in his own heir? What neglect on his part — lack of a loving example, lack of wisdom — brought his son to the commission of such a sin? Because it *is* a sin in the eyes of pious men.

He, Eliezar, is a stranger in Egypt. Is there any place where he will not feel like an exile? The houses where he lives with his people — supplied with every necessity, but furnished in utter simplicity — are like the dwellings of nomads, tents in a desert which are set up and taken down from day to day. The treasures which he has gathered, thanks to his foresight and his talents as a merchant, he doesn't consider to be really his — he only administers them, gives them away to the needy, uses them to help support people and opinions which he — his eye sharpened by chess-playing — sees as progressive, as representing a victory over sluggishness of mind and weakness of will. Now as he lies in the darkness, he is overcome by doubt, a lifelong enemy: is this perhaps pride, the chessplayer's love for plotting the future, the pleasure of working out possible solutions, reached through a series of bold calculations?

Because of his mother, the young Klafthi belongs forever to the others, not to the People. Eliezar has never doubted the precision of the Law. And yet . . . the word "slave" will never cross his lips in connection with that child. He can't even think it. The overseer, a freedman, assumes that the boy who has been entrusted to him belongs to his own caste. The boy himself knows nothing; he accepts his place and his surroundings as a matter of course . . . . But is that really true? Whenever Eliezar is on the estate, his eyes search the grounds until somewhere — near the stables, or outside the wall with the watch towers, in the orchard — he discovers that tanned figure, swift as water. The superintendent's clerk has said more than once that the boy can think as fast as he can run; he learned to read and write with as much ease as if he were playing a game.

Behind Eliezar's closed eyelids appears the fleeting gleam of white porticos, the long galleries of the schools of Alexandria. The desire to develop an unformed mind — is that pride? to be able to put in charge of the estate, which holds no interest for his legitimate heir, a young administrator, a child of the country who values the land ... To glide through the reeds in the dahabyah in the cool of the evening under a yellow-rose sky and listen to a trusted voice next to him reporting on harvests and flocks . . . Is it pride to want to think about the future? Is it better to do nothing, to let matters drift, to wait passively to see what will happen to the boy: a servant in the striped shirt of a fellaheen, working the land, rowing the dahabyah, who might one day, consumed by an uneasiness he doesn't understand, run off to become a thief or an assassin?

Standing in the darkness, his eyes fixed on the luminous blue rectangle of the gauze-curtained open door, Eliezar pushes these questions aside, cleanses himself spiritually before the Divine Presence, utters the Shema for peace through the night.

Perhaps it is the light falling over the meandering black and white pattern of the mosaics — suddenly the image rises before the Prefect of a chessboard divided into black and white squares, and a hand cautiously shifting the carved ivory figures, one by one. An echo of words spoken long ago in a house in Alexandria, in a space dominated by a silver candlestick with seven branches . . .

His own voice, too loud in the stillness, expresses what was for him the conclusion of the conversation that had just ended. "It is we who rule the world."

The other's silence lasts until he takes a chess piece out of play. Then the ironic question: "*We?*"

Hadrian can never understand or tolerate this constant need for precise consideration of the fine points of Roman status. In spite of the favor bestowed upon him by Rome, in spite of the prestige and official citizenship of his family — which has served the Empire with honor for several generations

— he feels himself to be a Roman of the second rank, compared with the Romans of Rome. This man opposite him, with his tired eyes and soft voice, has no aspirations, for himself or his kinfolk, to what the Christianized Egyptian Hadrian considers the highest honor; he doesn't mock Hadrian, but he seems to detract from his identification as a proper Latin, to which he has a right through his upbringing, his outlook, and above all, his recent appointment.

After that first noteworthy working visit to the estate in the Delta, an unusual relationship has developed between Hadrian and Eliezar ben Ezekiel — not friendship, even less a conventional exchange of courtesy visits (Hadrian goes to Eliezar, never the other way round).

His own motivations are not clear to Hadrian. Sometimes he is overcome by a certain uneasiness, a feeling that he is poised on the brink of an abyss: he feels compelled to sound its depths. But he always draws back from the decisive step. He does not pay his visits for business reasons; Eliezar fulfils his obligations with exemplary precision, satisfying all demands. What other points of contact do their lives have? As an Egyptian, a Christian and a Roman by preference, Hadrian feels a triple weight of distrust toward the Jew, mixed with wonder and secret aversion. His visits to Eliezar's house carry a touch of self-torment and at the same time seem necessary to slake a nameless, growing curiosity. What is he seeking? Why?

Hadrian cannot play the Indian game — with two groups of ivory figures on a board with black and white squares — which Eliezar keeps within reach of his hand. He doesn't see the sense of it: why a complicated system of related shapes, conjuring problems over and over again out of nothing? The Egyptian finds frivolity and the pursuit of profit understandable (and objectionable) reasons for playing games, but what delight can there be in seeking solutions to endlessly repeated problems?

Eliezar never receives his guest in the family circle, but always in the quiet austere chamber where the only signs of personal taste are the chessboard and the seven-branched candlestick. In spite of this reserve, Hadrian senses vaguely from the other's manner, something which is never put into words but which they have in common. It is this which drives Hadrian at intervals — under some pretext or other which is always courteously accepted — to pay his visits to Eliezar's house.

At that first non-working visit, questions are asked casually, answered casually, about the outcome of the incident in the canefields. Order has been restored, that kind of mischievous behavior will not occur again. The boy who killed the cock has been sent away.

"An intelligent child — restless because he's so talented . . . I've sent him to school in the city; he has the makings of a teacher, a secretary, or at the least, a helpful administrator for my estate."

A quiet hint: no reason for doubt or uneasiness on the part of the official, who is always well-informed about the regulations promulgated by the Emperor Theodosius on the subject of pagan practices. Hadrian is no longer faced with the choice of guilt for ignoring a punishable act or of getting Eliezar into trouble. He wants to indicate in no uncertain terms (magistrates who ignore their duty in these matters commit a crime) to the Jew — who had taken justice into his own hands so quickly and with such self-assurance — that this has become a question of conscience. Hadrian therefore evokes the militant stance in matters of belief of Ambrosius, the Bishop of Milan, whose influence is felt beyond the court to the farthest corners of the Empire. Often Eliezar appears better informed than Hadrian himself, about what is happening in Constantinople and Milan.

They discuss politics — that is, Hadrian takes the floor, not only to broach a subject which passionately interests him, but also to look like even more of an authority — in short, a Roman — in the eyes of Eliezar who, while he listens, usually looks at the chessboard and from time to time moves a piece. The stream of words is directed against the other's slight reactions. Hadrian has difficulty establishing a connection between what he is saying and the older man's rare responses: a smile, a frown, a thoughtful look, a sorrowful closing of the eyes. Has he ever secretly hoped to catch Eliezar in opinions which would be considered unacceptable by the pious Emperor Theodosius and his powerful bishops?

Later, thinking back on these visits, Hadrian realizes that on questions of domestic and foreign policy, Eliezar prefers to analyze the present situation rather than express an opinion about objectives. He never uses the words "divine" or "august" when he speaks of the Emperor, but praises Theodosius's zest for work, dependability and family feeling. There is always a noticeable strain of skepticism which the young official finds extremely provoking. Does that elusive reserve hide a seed of rebellion, a danger to Rome? He tries to get a hold on Eliezar's political opinions; his picture of them is alternately black and white, like the squares on the chessboard.

Shreds of conversation, submerged for thirty years, rise in Hadrian's memory while he stares at the black and white marble floors of the prefecture. He remembers some things which he himself had said and what Eliezar had replied, or implied. There was the question of the appointment of Flavius Stilicho to the supreme command of the army. As an Egyptian by birth, Hadrian could hardly take the liberty of openly criticizing the elevation to the highest military post of someone who was of half-Greek, half-Vandal descent. Since he had only recently become a Christian himself, Hadrian could not look down on the Christianized Stilicho.

Because of his irrational aversion to the streak of Northern barbarism in the most powerful personality at the Imperial court, Hadrian entered into an alliance with those authorities in Alexandria who were hostile to Stilicho. A rumor was being bruited about that the liberal attitude of the new *Magister Militum* toward unbelievers had incurred the displeasure of Bishop Ambrosius. Eliezar had this reaction: "Flavius Stilicho is a diplomat and a man of integrity. His appointment is a counterbalance to the influence of incompetent or corrupt advisers."

Hadrian (tensely): Such as?

Eliezar (calmly): Let's say such as the *praefectus praetorio Orientis*.

"Rufinus?"

"Rufinus." (An enemy of Bishop Ambrosius and, in addition, a pagan Gaul. No possible objection there.)

Still another memory: a rebellion against the authorities in Thessalonica was punished, at Rufinus's insistence, by putting to the sword seven thousand inhabitants of the city after they were invited to the circus on the pretext of watching games. For this mass murder, Bishop Ambrosius laid a severe penance on the Emperor. When Hadrian praised this action of the Church, Eliezar looked away: "Whoever is guilty can't be free: a man is like wax in the hands of those who know what evil he has done."

A new flash of memory: there was news that Christians at Callinicum, on the Persian border, had destroyed a synagogue. Emperor Theodosius gave orders that the criminals should be punished and the

Jewish community fully compensated. But Bishop Ambrosius forced the Emperor to annul these measures, arguing that to tolerate Jews is to persecute Christians. When Hadrian mentions this, Eliezar does not react. His sharp-featured face looks ashen in the reflection of his purple caftan; his eyes are filled with shadows. Suddenly he begins to talk about Flavius Stilicho, a solitary man in the most responsible post in the Empire, unimpeachable, capable, prudent. "A man who is the object of hatred and threats because he won't allow anyone to manipulate him. He is indispensable as no one else is . . ."

Nevertheless, Hadrian does not feel more sympathetic to the barbarian — on the contrary.

Gradually, he has begun to talk persistently about religious questions—specifically the new laws against idolatry and heresy, hoping to trap the Jew into reactions that will confirm his own belief that he, Hadrian, alone knows the truth. But from the first, he faces an impenetrable wall. Like a mirror or a sounding-board, Eliezar echoes what Hadrian says, or is silent insofar as his silence does not become discourteous.

"In the name of Jesus Christ our Redeemer who died on the Cross for our sins," Hadrian, time and again, curses the worship of Serapis, who has been the god of the city of Alexandria since the time of the Ptolemies; he describes in profuse detail what goes on in that irritatingly gaudy temple, which is as impregnable as a fortress: loathsome orgies, debauchery between men, infant sacrifice.

Eliezar: That's what they say. It's never been proven.

Hadrian: All the priests are castrated or perverted, a clique of so-called initiates in the secrets of Serapis as god of the underworld, who practice magic, call up spirits . . . It appears that a goodly number of young students are involved in this scandalous situation.

Eliezar: Those sorts of temples preserve very old traditions of knowledge. Remember that the unfamiliar and incomprehensible always rouse fear and distrust.

Hadrian *(angry at the other's conciliatory attitude; naturally, Eliezar doesn't have to worry about it)*: There's a stinking ulcer at the heart of Alexandria. When will that be burned away?

Eliezar: Violence is pointless.

Hadrian: In the battle of Good against Evil, we don't talk about violence — it's a sacred struggle.

3.

Fragmented memories, like bubbles rising from the depths of a marsh. Whatever is fermenting on the bottom is hidden from Hadrian. He knows only the surface of the conversations with Eliezar which he remembers now. It is impossible to tell what thoughts were going through Eliezar's head as he bent over the chessboard. But perhaps this:

Who can dare to believe that he can checkmate the evil in the world? The "Savior": those who follow him imagine that they are "redeemed". Pride, pride, but dressed in deceptively humble garments. As if it could have been given to mortal man to settle accounts miraculously, in the space of a moment, with the powers of darkness. The Nazarene did not act wisely when he preached a doctrine that most people would misunderstand. He himself knew the full significance — would he otherwise have spoken in parables?

71

He has split Judaism into two camps; those who respect the Law and know all things come in their own time and demand their own price — including the fulfillment of our hopes — and those who covet salvation, who cannot wait, who desire redemption, who refuse to admit that each of us, fully aware of our own limitations, must, alone and unyielding, regenerate our alliance with the Eternal. Good and Evil are inherent in human nature, indissolubly bound up with conscience. Knowledge of evil, or even complicity in it, is the price man must pay for his sense of morality. This imposes the heaviest responsibility, demands the greatest humility. To be a Jew is to know that being chosen also means suffering beneath the full weight of evil, which must multiply a thousandfold before human insight into these things is accomplished. And to be fully aware of this always, never to forget it, is the essence of justice itself.

To be "redeemed" — it means to be able to enjoy the privileges of the human condition while being at the same time as innocent, as irresponsible, as the beasts of the field. To worship a Redeemer — it means wanting to serve two masters, to be half man, half animal, relieved of the burden of guilt and sorrow created by our own imperfection. To go on living halfway between the unthinking acceptance of the state of nature and the assurance of having been made in the image of God.

I can never deny that through the Nazarene's teaching a desire for inner perfection has taken root in the pagan world. But the way in which the doctrine lends itself to a fusion with idolatry and with many kinds of interpretation, the way it has given itself up to an encroaching sectarianism — that is completely alien to me. The faith of my forefathers is determined in itself, unflinching, impenetrable: the only place for Israel is within the boundaries of the Law. Under the delusion that the Writings ordered it, the Nazarene has propagated the faith as if it were a sponge soaking up indiscriminately everything into which it is dipped.

Now take this Hadrian, a man who has

not been shaped by a long tradition of observance of an immutable law. Centuries of superstition are in his blood, blind fear of the beast in men which must be exorcised by magic; awe before the secrets of reincarnation represented by Isis and Osiris; the desire to solve the mysteries of heaven and hell which are propounded by the cult of Serapis... he finally encumbers himself with badly digested book knowledge borrowed from a dozen philosophers and poets. Discontented, filled with insecurity, he longs to quell the chaos in himself. In Christianity, he obviously finds satisfaction for all the good will that is in him, and consolation and hope where insight into himself is impossible or intolerable. Evil is in him no longer; he believes himself to be saved; all around him he sees forms he can combat, cross in hand.

He wants to be a Roman with the cross in his hand: a man of action, convinced of his mission to impose laws upon others. There are no Romans more fanatical than those from outside Rome who have been converted to the Empire; the greater the distance they have come, the more intense their fervor.

This Hadrian: a man still young, in the prime of his life. Roughly the same age as my son. I hardly understand my son; I have little patience with him. But despite all his shortcomings and weaknesses, he is a warm-blooded man and his standards are human standards. More interested in possessions and profit than in treasures of wisdom, shrewd and businesslike, passionate, sensual. But he knows himself. He doesn't pretend to be better than he is — the opposite in every way to this Egyptian who is so proud of his piety and integrity, whose contempt for the body and the senses stems from his own secret fear and guilt. He goes out of his way to let it be known that he lives without women and holds fast to the precepts of his faith which forbid sinful thoughts. I have seldom met a man so troubled with desires which he doesn't dare to acknowledge. Seldom, too, a more ambitious man, or one with so many pretensions. What do I have in common with him? Why does *he* seek my company when I cannot even talk with my own son?

4.

The Prefect no longer sees the black and white of the floor of the justice hall. Claudius Claudianus. The little Egyptian, Klafthi. The thin brown boy caught in the act of sacrifice among the reeds, grown up to be a student in a toga. Encountered again by accident in the galleries of Alexandria, walking behind a baldheaded teacher of rhetoric. Later, the objections, the self-doubt: is it fitting for a high official, having just had a short conversation with the philosopher and orator Claudianus (a living encyclopedia of art and good taste) — is it fitting for the high official then to address some words equally to one of the philosopher's pupils? Does one recognize an inferior in another man's household, a protege whose background and status are obscure?

A trace of a smile appears on Eliezar's lips when Hadrian tells him about the encounter. Then he says brusquely, "A brilliant student — or so I've heard. No, I never see him. He lives with the rhetorician."

How long — or how soon — after that came those chaotic days when, under the tutelage of Theophilus, Bishop of Alexandria, the temple of Serapis was stormed and destroyed? Later, witnessing the proceedings against one of the wealthy patrons of the temple (suspected of complicity in certain obscene rites, traces of which have been discovered, supposedly, in the vaults under the debris), Hadrian recognizes once more the student Klafthi among the proteges of this Olympiodorus. Klafthi's face is narrower, harder; all traces of boyishness have vanished from it, but there remains, more strongly, that look of dark defiance which had struck the Prefect in the canefields. That precise quality — a fleeting waft of wildness and turbidity from the sinking world of paganism — fills Hadrian with dismay and confusion.

Toward Olympiodorus and the handful of unmistakable catamites of his following, he feels nothing but abhorrence; he considers any fate too good for them and hopes that they will receive the most merciless punishment. But he is less sure about Klafthi. Disturbed, upset, he goes to Eliezar to tell him about the situation.

But when it becomes apparent that Eliezar already knows everything, and has known it for a considerable time — the death of the tutor Claudianus, the evil friendships, the temptations of luxury and licentiousness — Hadrian can no longer contain himself. He bursts out: "And you haven't taken him away from that? You made no attempt to control him? A member of your household, a subordinate, a foster child — what is he exactly? — delivered over to the heathen?"

Transported by emotion (Compassion? Christian charity?) he paints the corruption that he sees as a poisonous aura surrounding that clique; his agitation grows as he feels Eliezar's deathly quiet, dark eyes on his face.

"Didn't you do anything for him? After the incident with the cock, you rewarded him, in a manner of speaking, by offering him an expensive education at the best schools in the city. All right, good — I didn't say anything. That was defensible — he remained in your service, you took the responsibility. But now you're willing to put up with *this*?"

Eliezar (stiffly): Apparently I gave him the opportunity to play a more dangerous game than the sacrifice of a cock. But he chose those friends, that life, himself. He's no longer a child.

"But isn't he still under your authority? Doesn't he still owe you obedience?"

Eliezar makes a tired gesture of rejection. "I have

no control over his inclinations. I let him do as he wishes. After all, he's nothing to me."

"He's in danger now of being tried together with Olympiodorus and his circle."

"Anyone who wants to, may take a hand in his destiny."

Hadrian personally intercedes for this lost sheep, takes pity on him, takes him into service as his secretary. When, after a long time, he visits Eliezar once more, he says he believes that he has presented an example of Christian charity, and that he has reaped rewards from it. Without exaggerating, he can praise the character and accomplishment of the young man, whose name he has latinized to Claudius. Claudius's Greek is perfect. He composes excellent letters. He has an obvious literary gift. He writes strikingly beautiful verses and recites them with talent.

"So. A Greek," Eliezar says; he shrugs, fixing Hadrian with a sad, searching look. "A little Egyptian Greek — there are so many in Alexandria. Does he practice Greek customs too?"

Hadrian stiffens. He hurries to hide his discomfort under a flood of words.

"Every day his Latin gains in force and finesse. He would have an assured future, even in Rome."

"As an Egyptian Roman then?"

Hadrian, suspecting hidden meanings behind these words, is stubbornly determined to show this skeptic that a soul is capable of change, that base instincts may be overcome.

Time passes. Claudius — who prefers to be called Claudianus in honor of the rhetorician with whom he studied — gradually becomes well known in literary circles. Hadrian's visits to Eliezar become less frequent. Each time he comes, he offers to bring Claudius with him, but each time Eliezar refuses. He has sat for a long time over a much-admired work of Claudius's, the *Gigantomachia*, which Hadrian gave him to read. In masterly language, it presents a vision of the sound and fury of the Titans, the ancient inhabitants of the earth, who rebelled against the gods.

Eliezar has never seen the boy since that day when he had stared from the dahabyeh across the water at his bloody palms. He might have brushed past him a hundred times in the streets and parks of Alexandria, may even have looked into his face without recognizing him.

His praise of the poet's work is measured; he is aware that Hadrian is watching him. One line haunts him: "I shall never hesitate to become the weapon which brings Zeus to destruction."

When someone is being long sought in the jungle, his footprints and other clues like broken branches tell what sort of start he has had and what direction he is taking. In the same way, Eliezar proceeds — in silent doubt — to read, in the secret language of themes and word choice, the history of a rebellion which is ignorant of its own roots.

He congratulates Hadrian on the results of his intercession and begs to be left in solitude. For some time now he has suffered attacks of sharp pain which the doctors have not been able to relieve.

When, some months later, Hadrian visits once more he is struck by the disturbing alteration in Eliezar's appearance: this man, who had once been straight as an arrow, sits huddled in the folds of his garments; he is emaciated, withered; his eyes are glassy. The conversation doesn't flow. After some hesitation (the subject now seems inappropriate), Hadrian reads aloud a new poem by his protégé about the Phoenix — dying, its eyes frosted over (Eliezar nods imperceptibly), it mounts its burning nest, which will be both its grave and its cradle:

> In a single flight he soars, the son
> from the father
> Who has begotten himself: between life
> and life
> Only brief torment: a threshold of fire.

Eliezar sits without moving, his averted face in shadow.

Reports: Emperor Theodosius has moved his household from Constantinople to Milan. Administrative reforms are imminent, officials are being summoned from all the corners of the Empire. New appointments have been made. Hadrian is among the privileged; news about his merits and his religious zeal has reached the ears of the Emperor — and his Archbishop. A post awaits him overseas, at the Northern court, where he will exercise the function of *Magister Officiorum.*

He prepares to take ship shortly with his staff and his retinue. A last visit to Eliezar: a last goodbye, both of them know it. Eliezar hands him a paper, a copy of a clause in his will: "*Klafthi servus meus liberesto. . .* that my slave Klafthi shall be free. . . ."

"This will become legal in the hour of my death.

My heirs will not be able to claim him. Don't say anything to him about this. Promise me. He has never been treated like a slave."

Hadrian is assailed by mixed emotions. Something in him shrinks back, hides itself at the thought that — if he had known — he could have bought the boy from Eliezar, that the jewel of his personal staff, whom everyone in Alexandria envies, could have been his inalienable possession.

Eliezar senses the other man's inner turmoil; for Klafthi-Claudius's sake, he wants no misunderstanding about the nature of his benevolence and the reason for it. He gestures for silence with his sallow, bony hand and begins wearily to say what has to be said.

After the confession he does not give Hadrian a chance to react. The decision has been pronounced but more arrangements must be made.

"In his interest, don't tell anyone that he's a freedman. It's only as a free-born man that he can have the future he deserves. That holds true everywhere, but especially in Rome. He's a poet, not a clerk. Introduce him into illustrious houses where his gifts will do him justice. I'm thinking of the Anicii — there are two young men in that family who

I have heard are going to receive the highest honor. Let him become their protégé. You've made a half-Roman of him — now complete your work. He must not come back to Alexandria. And now one other thing, the last thing that I shall ask of you: swear by everything that you hold most sacred, Hadrian, that he will never hear about his relationship to me and mine."

Under the spell of those lackluster eyes, Hadrian raises his right hand: I swear. . . .

In the dream, the ship vanished behind the horizon. Whoever abandoned him there had sailed away out of his life, forever. The Prefect has only to close his eyes to stand once more on the marble steps, to hear again the whisper of the wavelets as they come to lick the steps and retreat, leaving a fringe of foam meandering about the tips of his shoes.

Just as the sea, in deepening layers of greens and violet, suddenly becomes an abyss — so those who explore their pasts find, in their memories, chasms of unsuspected darkness.

Silence at his back, the loneliness of the narrow colonnade along the precipice. In his dream, he was aware, even without seeing it, of the fragment carved in the rock behind him — a hand raised in the gesture: I swear . . .

The Prefect forces himself to open his eyes, to look directly at the tangible objects of the here and now — the row of empty chairs, for example, opposite him along the wall; the bronze lamps on their pedestals, the patches of glaring daylight behind the arched openings of the windows.

"I swear that I shall pass judgment in the spirit of the law."

At dawn, before the hearing began, he had spoken these words, the customary oath taken by every magistrate who acts as justice; he had, for perhaps the thousandth time, raised his right hand.

5.

Now as then — thinks the man who calls himself Niliacus — now as then I am condemned to silence. Then, ten years ago, I was silent (or rather, I didn't deny that I had sacrificed a cock) because otherwise suspicion would have fallen on my benefactor and friend Mallius Theodorus, who had in fact done it. *Now* I'm silent about Marcus Anicius Rufus (who perhaps had, perhaps hadn't, been about to sacrifice a cock) so that his relationship with me won't make his burden heavier.

With his face turned toward the wall of the holding room reserved for the humble (after the reading of the record of evidence he had been separated from the patricians), he laughs, a grimace of self-mockery. He hadn't been able to stop himself from posing a riddle to the Prefect, from sowing confusion in that brain, to leave an impression there which would stimulate further investigation. Why? For the first time in ten years, he finds himself once again face to face with this foolish, this arrogant pedant. He has hardly changed, Hadrian — his hair somewhat thinner, somewhat greyer, his mouth more compressed than ever, always wavering between affability and disapproval. He plays with his signet ring as he played with it then. No trace of recognition in his look (of course I have decidedly changed) but signs of disquiet, uncertainty, irritation.

The man must have a boundless capacity for self-delusion. Indefatigable in pursuit of his enemies, those who don't think like him. . . He imagines he smells heresy, high treason, even when the air is pure. Always a morbid urge to humiliate those whom he suspects of lacking respect for his own perfection. He has hated Marcus Anicius Rufus since the day twenty-five years ago, when he obtained for me — a budding little poet — a post with real Romans, real aristocrats.

The soldier posted at the door begins to stir, his attention caught perhaps by the immobile figure of the accused who sits with his back turned. The man who calls himself Niliacus turns to face forward again on his bench, stares before him at the filthy, defaced marble of the opposite wall.

Hadrian, the light of Egypt — he was far from being the disinterested protector whom he pretended to be. He had no sympathy, no joy over his protege's swift rise — on the contrary. The first time he did

what he intended, his interference (Slander? Half-
truths? Colored account of a past that even he never
really knew?) cost me my friendship with the Anicii.
Then came the return of the prodigal son; at least
that was the impression he wanted to give. But was
Hadrian's inclination the same as fatherly love?

The marble of the wall, discolored, red-brown and
yellow, makes one think of sick flesh. What is going
on in his head, Hadrian, now Prefect of the City:
does he crave money, property, and above all,
authority, because he cannot completely possess
certain people, because he cannot impose his will on
them? He demands lifelong gratitude, tries to hold
a man fast in exchange for one past favor, even when
the relationship has been outgrown — that's worse
than stupidity, that's an outrage!

How refreshing and interesting, above all, how
charitable and open-minded — compared to *his*
phrases and platitudes — did I find the gruff, often
irritable manner of Mallius Theodorus there in the
North — a really learned and well-read man — and
devoid of any trace of vanity or ambition. The
epigram in which I compared the two of them —
the uncorruptible dreamer versus the meddling
insomniac — was a mistake, caused by the desperate

wish to be free, to prick his thick skin — violently, if need be. Four lines, no more; they all but cost Mallius his life — and cost me more, in another sense. For having written them, the rising poet — which I was then — had begun to weave his own destiny.

I didn't think about that jingle for a long time after I wrote it, and for a long time after I was elevated above the crowd of Mallius's connections and entered Stilicho's powerful retinue. Hadrian — in the meantime dispatched from Milan to Rome under the pretext of a promotion — apparently always carried within himself this injury to his vanity like an open running wound, which would never heal.

In the marble of the wall, a confusion of threads and reddish spots, like exposed bloody tissue.

Ten years ago, only a short distance from here, somewhere in a subterranean vault, seized by desperation and rage, I smashed my fist against the wall. Not because of the sentence I could expect when I let myself be accused of *sacrificium* and *divinatio*. . . but at the certainty that no one — not Stilicho, not Mallius, not the Anicii, not a living soul in Rome or anywhere — would risk his own skin for me or think of me as anything but a useful instrument, amusing company, an interesting connection — now, alas, unfortunately led astray.

6.

Imprisoned between sea and rock without a way out — for he could not follow whoever was calling from afar. The memory of the fear he had felt in his dream fills the Prefect with discomfort. He stands up, walks quickly back and forth; he can't lose his shadow — the room is filled with the invisible past. The last visit with the condemned man then, ten years ago, a visit prompted by the need to explicate in detail why, after the cruel offense which he, Hadrian, had sustained, he was forced to undermine, systematically, the other's reputation.

Suddenly the face of the man opposite him — exhausted and dirty after days of detention — flamed with a fierce look which Hadrian had never been able to forget:

"I *have* — haven't I — asked for forgiveness publicly, in a poem, so that everyone would know about it. An apology in good and proper form. I've cringed at your feet like a suppliant. Isn't that enough?"

Hadrian: What can I do with that? It comes too late. You cannot undo the measureless damage you have caused me with that epigram. I can't undo the fact that all of Rome now knows who and what you are: a Jew's freed slave — and most important — found by me in the most dissolute pagan clique in Alexandria. I spared you during the proceedings. I didn't mention your real name or reveal your background — nothing about that will find its way into the documents. It would be impossible for me to show you greater leniency. Out of respect for your merit as a poet that silence is accepted, but everyone knows the truth and those who prize the favors of court and authorities and value a spotless reputation, have forgotten that they ever opened their doors to you or applauded your verses.

The unspoken words behind this speech, carefully suppressed out of self-preservation: "I have heard your pleas. Not because they were full of pathos or because you compared me to Alexander, Achilles or Hercules. Not even because you acknowledged my authority before the whole world. Two words have touched me, have roused compassion in me for you: *misererer tuorum* . . . Have pity upon those whom you own. Because of these two words, I open my doors to you anew, I offer my protection anew. So you know that you have never received more attention from anyone; no one has ever shown you more affection. I will do my utmost to free you."

Hadrian did not say these words. Distrust and fear paralyzed his tongue. Distrust: How much of what Claudius said was sincere — how much was just rhetoric and poetic exaggeration? What were Claudius's real feelings? Fear: if he said these words to Claudius, wouldn't Hadrian be revealing too much, wouldn't he be giving himself away? He had no desire to throw off the mask. He could not bear the possible consequences. He stood to lose social standing — he might even have to quit Rome. And there was also the danger that Claudius would reject him, that he would lose Claudius forever.

The lighthouse of Pharos: a warning finger on the horizon, the vanishing coastline of Egypt. On the ship's after-deck, overcome with emotion (at the leave-taking but even more at the fulfillment of his most fervent wishes: first Rome, then Imperial Milan and advancement), Hadrian swore silently at that time to let the young man at his side share in his glory — as a son, as a brother; to serve the unfolding of his talent, to elevate the soul of the heathen — an indispensable condition to the noble harmony between the two of them.

The Prefect starts up, jarred from his reliving of the past. His clerks, his officers, the herald have made their entrance and taken their places again. How much time has passed since he ordered a pause so that he could examine the confiscated library? He is still not prepared to resume the hearing. They can wait.

He repairs to the room where he holds private conversations. Some staircases and galleries separate him from Niliacus there in the holding room. He knows that he has only to issue an order to the praetorian who has accompanied him and who waits now by the open door. And then? When the man appears before him, huddled in his threadbare mantle?

Hadrian summons Aulus Fronto, the Commander of the City guard. He brings news of what is happening in the dungeons below.

The slave Milo has admitted under pressure that on the evening of the man Niliacus's first visit to Marcus Anicius Rufus, he — on the latter's orders — gave the former a book roll from the library which this Niliacus took away with him.

"What text?"

"No text. A blank paper."

"What then? Go on."

"It appears that on the day of the entry of our august Emperor Honorius, Marcus Anicius Rufus was protecting the man who calls himself Niliacus from the City security service after he damaged a statue in the Forum of Trajan."

"What statue?"

"Of the poet Claudius Claudianus."

The Prefect is silent for a long time. Finally, still seated, he says, "Bring the mime Pylades and his dwarf. Not in the justice hall. *Here.*"

7.

With a grimace, Urbanilla thrusts herself away from the gate behind which Marcus Anicius Rufus's wife has just passed on her way to the hearing.

"Stuck-up bitch!"

"Shut up," hisses the dwarf. Now in his Priapus costume in the clear light of day, he looks like nothing so much as a walking cucumber with a red top or an enormous stuffed sausage. He cannot take off the outfit because he has nothing on underneath, not even a loincloth; his face is shiny with sweat; he curses and rubs himself against the wall.

Urbanilla stretches; her naked breasts, with painted nipples, tremble under the five rows of cheap gilt strings. From the corner of her eye she can still see, in the distance, Sempronia at the door which opens onto the galleries of the hall of justice. A matron wearing the same ceremonial dress she had worn when she had received her guests twelve hours earlier, as much in control of herself in the halls of the prefecture as in her own *triclinium*. Urbanilla mimics the gait of the patrician lady and doubles over with soundless laughter, her hands on her hips.

"Looks like sour grapes to me.   Her style – you'll have it when chickens have teeth. Balcho, give the bitch a kick."

"If you've got the balls to come near me, Fatso, I'll scratch your eyes out."

"Listen to her – the goddess Ariadne! Get away, you stink of the fishmarket!"

"It's your disgusting hide you're talking about – that's what's closest to your nose!"

The leader, Pylades, lying full-length on a camp bed, kicks off his stained, wrinkled stage cloak. "Shut your mouth, trash, idiot good-for-nothing. . . ."

The dwarf comes rolling up to him as quickly as his costume will permit to pick up the covering and spread it carefully over the actor's feet. "Why is it that all at once I'm not good enough for you any more? You're ashamed to appear with me. You don't need me."

"Stop your drivel, I've had enough! It's not normal for them to keep us waiting such a damned long time."

"The two of us – Bacchus and Priapus – we have to stay together and do our ventriloquist number – that's always a success. . . . What good do *they* do us

— that cheap whore and Balcho, that fat ball of grease, stupid as the hind end of a pig — the only thing he knows how to do is gorge himself. We did so well for each other with our own acts —"

"*Our* acts? Everything you do you've learned from me. You're nothing, you don't know anything, I pulled you out from under the bridges . . ."

"I'm not grateful enough to you for that? Don't I do everything — all you need to do is ask? I'm your doormat, your dog. Now you want to tell me to go to hell?"

"Don't whine! You know what I have against you. Don't meddle with things that don't concern you. *I* give the orders here. No one told you that this time we needed an extra one."

"But I thought you had the schoolmaster in mind for the goings-on outside in the fresh air, boss. I swear —"

"You're lying! I had completely different plans, and you just can't swallow that. You wanted to get him out of the way. That damned venom of yours could cost us our heads. He's not a tramp; he's not an illiterate or a runaway slave or a backward yokel who lets himself be led like a cow to the slaughter. How did you get it in your head —"

"But we had to bring the altar and the cocks . . ."

"That was enough in this case. I had my arrangements."

"This fellow got on your nerves — admit it, boss."

"I said that he was hard to catch but I'm damned if that isn't better than sickly jealous toadying. Anyway, I was just beginning to get a hold on him . . . with him I could have staged something entirely different from these miserable shows where I run a big risk because of your dangerous stubbornness. Now he can get us into deep trouble."

"I swear that I haven't let anything slip. He doesn't know anything. I haven't talked to him, I only sent him a message through a third person supposed to come from Marcus Anicius Rufus — it was to lure him into the garden. . . . If they make him confess the story of the anonymous message, we're protected and the Prefect will be satisfied. He'll be able to send all the lords into exile. It won't be the first time it's happened like this . . ."

"Idiot, you want to make everything too pretty! Don't you realize what it means to be summoned a second time, to be subjected to a new interrogation — this has never happened before! There's something behind it. The Prefect is suspicious, he's interested in this man who apparently hasn't revealed anything about himself — and he's given a false name too. And you choose the moment when it's in our interest to know as little as possible about him — you choose that moment to throw out information about him — to tell where he lives, what he does and exactly what we said to him. Do you imagine that the Prefect will show mercy to informers who don't understand their business? We're in for it!"

"What then? What then, Pylades?" pleads the dwarf, now in tears.

The giant Balcho steps out of his corner and runs his hand with lightning speed across his throat, accompanying the gesture with a death-rattle. Urbanilla, screaming with laughter, points at the dwarf. She cannot quiet down. From behind the distant gate a soldier of the watch orders them to be silent.

8.

Urbanilla, child of the City. She cannot remember her parents. She has always lived in the streets, under the bridges or the arches of the aquaducts, roaming from one district to another with groups of homeless people — mostly freed slaves from the provinces come to seek work in Rome; refugees from bordering territories taken over by barbarians; every kind of beggar. There are hundreds of children like her: cast out, left behind, run away, orphaned. Living among grownups, a skittish, hardened mob — street-wise, quick-fingered, with sharp nails and teeth. Their ranks are always being thinned through sickness and accidents; deformed children are seized at once by beggars; the cleverest and most agile end up sooner or later in groups of thieves or bands of acrobats. Half-grown boys and ripening maidens face other dangers: the slave market, the bordello, the press-gang for sailors.

Urbanilla knows all the blind alleys and lanes of the Subura quarter, all the hiding places in the hills bordering the city and along the banks of the Tiber. In bad weather she found shelter in sewers, warehouses, cellars, or in the open air in ditches, behind bushes or in the arcades of forbidden abandoned temples. She stole her food from street stalls, searched through rubbish for scraps.

She does not know how old she is, nor how she came by her name. She first menstruated at the time the Goths attacked the City. During the famine, she was one of those who knew how to hold their own ground without mercy. Like a rat, a ferret, a fierce, nervous beast of prey, she crawled, crept and climbed to reach her goal, kicking and biting anyone who tried to share her plunder or grab at her. In the chaos that followed the invasion by Alaric's troops she was separated from her teenaged companions. Whenever she ventured too close to the barbarian camp (looking for food which she believed was plentiful there), she was raped by everyone who could get hold of her.

After the barbarians departed, she huddled again, now here, now there, with the bands of vagrants — until the day when, in a pit behind the City wall, she gave birth to a child that did not live long because she could neither feed it nor care for it. A beggar woman, an herb-gatherer, helped her end a second and a third pregnancy.

The ruins were green again; new buildings rose on burned-out patches of land. In her torn shirt, Urbanilla sauntered past the taverns, looking to catch customers; she was not choosy. When the dwarf stopped her and offered money, she had to shriek with laughter at his audacity and the absurdity of the situation, but she went along.

A man in multicolored clothing, whom the dwarf treated respectfully — he called himself the master mime — promised her a life without worries if she was willing to "perform" with him whenever he wanted her to, in rich people's villas. For the first time, real shelter — a bed, meals, visits to the public baths. While the dwarf struck a cymbal or plucked a zither, Urbanilla danced the steps her master had taught her. Now, made-up, her hair tinted, curled and carefully coiffed, she played the roles of goddesses and nymphs — of whom she had never heard and whose names she could scarcely remember — before continually changing audiences which were sometimes bored, sometimes drunk, or watching in breathless excitement as the master (Bacchus, Jupiter — all of Olympus) leapt upon her.

The dwarf hates her and the large fat fellow who acts as aide and bodyguard would be delighted to get his paws on her, but does not dare and won't get the chance either. For her part, Urbanilla spits on the fat one, is afraid of the dwarf (although she doesn't let that show) and feels uncomfortable with her employer's indifferent distaste.

Who cares anything about how she lives? She's nobody, a leaf on a tree, a pebble in the riverbed, a creature without rights. Only the here and now exist for her. The street is her domain, the only place where she really feels at home. Restless, inquisitive, quick to react, she becomes one of the crowd, and runs with them whenever there is anything to see, inspects all the merchandise in the stalls without buying anything, takes part in all street scuffles and manages to run away at the right moment, without worrying about the decent clothes she has been wearing since she joined Pylades's troupe — cape and robe and veil.

Her face is the face of an alleycat, pale brown, triangular, with wide cheekbones, bright hungry eyes, small pointed teeth. Her body is wiry and voluptuous at the same time; her ribs can be counted, but she has round breasts. In repose, resting nonchalantly on one hip, she reveals the curves of her loins and belly, but she has the arms and legs of a hardened fighter and climber. Even in the garments which befit her new position as actress, she looks slovenly: her black coiffure stringy, kohl smeared on her eyelids. Pylades has forbidden her to solicit and has placed her under the supervision of the publican Apicius. She lives above his cellar and helps in the kitchen on those days when the actor does not need her.

Urbanilla never thinks about herself or her fate. She knows so little that she does not realize that she has no talent for dancing or acting; she is unconscious of her real power, which is skilfully exploited by Pylades in the mime show: a unique mixture of savagery and perversity — sometimes as spontaneous as a child or as uninhibited as a bacchante, and then again docile as a house pet, languidly willing, a thing which allows itself to be formed and moulded.

When she can't be in the streets, she likes to squat in a corner or in an open doorway, listening to sounds from outside, instinctively drawn to the ebb and flow of life in that sea of houses. Even without seeing anything, merely by sniffing the odors or feeling the air move over her skin, she can tell what is happening in the alleys, the time of day, any ordinary or unusual event.

She cleans her teeth with a toothpick, combs the snarls out of her hair. Sometimes she just sits quietly, her arms crossed, her hands clutching her shoulders. The scent of open fields, blown on the wind from over the Tiber, stirs fleeting memories of the blackened fireplaces under the aqueduct, of the child she buried there, of the begging and whoring on the outskirts of Rome.

On the day of the entry of the Emperor Honorius (Apicius's vaulted cellars have been chock-full since sunrise), as she sets about frying the fish, stooping in the little space full of smoke and stink behind the brazier, the dwarf enters — followed by Balcho — to tell her maliciously that Pylades is sitting in the public house with a man whom they have picked up in the street.

"For you to dance with, little darling, a handsome boy. You're going to be able to play Eros and Psyche, Venus and Adonis —"

"Get out, if you don't want boiling oil in your mug. . ."

But as soon as she has ladled the sardines out of the pans, she runs behind them, wiping her palms on her tunic, shaking her head and shoulders to divide her greasy hair into strands, two in front and two behind.

Opposite Pylades at the table sits a drunken beggar, thin under his rags, staring absently into his beaker. Urbanilla, enraged at this trick, spits and swears at the tramp and flees back to her saucepans.

Later, with her sharp infallible instinct for scenting trouble, she perceives that the master and the dwarf Homullus don't see eye to eye; there is a difference of opinion between them which goes deeper than the ordinary squabble. She has known all along that the dwarf's officious behavior — acting as if he were the master's deputy and right hand — irritates Pylades. She knows too — she's not stupid — that there is more involved in the performance than she has been told.

The performances are regularly interrupted by the *vigiles*; the players, amid confusion and lamentation, are taken by torchlight to the prefecture. The girl and Balcho usually have to wait only a very short time at the gate before Pylades and the dwarf return from the upstairs room. She doesn't know what goes on upstairs there; she never asks. She has her suspicions but she doesn't care about it. For magistrates, officials, patricians, the whole apparatus of the state and all the institutions of authority, she feels only fear and contempt — nothing else.

There comes a day — not long after the incident in Apicius's tavern — when Pylades takes her aside and orders her to go and see a certain *Pro Se* or *Ignotus* in the Iulia tenement behind the Ten Taverns.

"A schoolmaster, a starveling, a poor devil of a fellow, but if I'm right, not yet a wholly extinct volcano. Play up to him, you know a handful of love tricks, I'll leave it to you. The rest is my business."

"The disgusting old fellow from the *popina?*"

"You could be surprised. Anyway, I haven't asked for your opinion. You just do as I say. And don't put on airs. You've had plenty of others!"

Sullen but resigned, Urbanilla goes on her way. She has to wait a long time in a dark corner of the third floor of a tenement house, full of flies, until, toward evening, the tenant comes home. He lights an oil lamp and looks at her over the flame in his hand, in silent annoyance. Urbanilla feels inexplicably overwhelmed by an urge to run away, to scream — not from fear but from a repugnance which goes beyond horror, a longing to change, to cease to exist, to be delivered from something invisible that clings to her.

In the closeness of that small room, by the flickering light of the little lamp, facing the unknown one whose eyes offer her no assurance about her own reactions, she experiences herself for the first time as an "I", alone and lost in strange, unfathomable depths. When the man rejects her, she stumbles hastily down the dark staircase to find her way back to the street.

Pylades shrugs in contempt at her failure.

"I thought that you could do one thing, at least. I was mistaken."

At daybreak Urbanilla plunges once more into the labyrinth of the Subura — not because she wants to repeat the unsuccesful attempt (had she really attempted anything?). She finds, next to the fruit market and not far from the bathhouse, the shed where — barely separated by a torn awning from the street bustle — a half dozen youths (in rags for the most part) are gathered under the guidance of the equally ragged *ludi magister*.

Urbanilla hangs about, looking on from a distance, moving closer to see better, trying to overhear what is being said. She doesn't know why she is doing it. In the following days, she repeats the foray, until Pylades orders her to prepare for an approaching performance.

In the cortege of those who were arrested after the raid on Marcus Anicius Rufus's villa, she recognizes that man. His presence increases the feeling she has of resentment and malice against Pylades, Homullus and Balcho. Something has gone wrong; she is filled with desperate hope.

II.

CLAUDIUS CLAUDIANUS

1.

The palanquin in which the Emperor Honorius was sitting had just gone by when somewhere in the crowd behind me, under the pine trees, the cry rose, "*Munera, munera!* . . . The games! The games!" For an instant, everyone seemed paralyzed. The endless procession of the Emperor's officials, in multicolored togas, slowed their pace and then a kind of shudder went through the crowd. I, too, turned insofar as that was possible, stretched my neck, but couldn't pinpoint any more than anyone else where those cries were coming from. I wouldn't have believed my ears if I hadn't been able to read, in the lifted faces about me, that sudden fierce attention, that air of expectancy one recognized from the arena. I was reminded of the sensation which used to overcome me whenever I had to work my way through the waiting crowds near the Circus. Tension, blood lust, the blind craving for diversion — all that gave off an odor more penetrating than the smell of sweat. Once again there was the undercurrent of excitement and desire which swirls and seethes, a phenomenon much more terrifying in a

115

human mob than in nature — at sea, for example, when a storm arises or in the clouded sky just before the first clap of thunder.

This didn't last longer than a few moments; then the praetorians formed a cordon to keep the spectators under control. The procession began to move once again. In the distance I saw Honorius — a glistening golden doll bobbing above the heads of his soldiers and bishops.

It was natural to think that those cries were the work of mischievous youths, or political enemies of the Emperor who were trying to rouse popular feeling against him by reminding everyone that he was responsible for the prohibition of an immensely popular public amusement. But for me, that hoarse cry of "*Munera! Munera!*" meant something entirely different from a real desire for the resumption of an unsavory and cruel exhibition. The priests who walked before Honorius with their crosses and banners, began to sing again, but where I stood, there still hung in the air an echo of the shriek of protest, of deathly fear — because that was what it was — stifled, as if it were coming from the old place, or from behind the bricked-up doors of the temples. These cries brought me to myself. I became conscious of time and place.

Fourteen years ago, I had walked behind Honorius over the very same pavement on the way to the Forum for his first ceremonial reception as Emperor in Rome. Then the City, elevated on its seven hills as if it were inviolable, had gleamed with marble and gilt. That was partly illusion. The obelisk, the galleries, the façades of the government buildings and, of course, the churches, were polished and richly decorated for the occasion. But in the temples, the statues of the gods were filthy and covered with cobwebs. I had a place of honor in the procession, where I walked with dignity in an embroidered tunic, in my hand the encased ode, calm, alert as always, self-assured and at the same time impressed because finally the City, the center of the world, had recovered her right to house the Emperor, to be the seat of court and government. I don't care for Milan with its raw winter wind, I detest Ravenna with its swamps.

As I walked in this bizarre procession — monks next to courtiers, armed barbarians side by side with senators — under the triumphal arches along the Clivus Capitolinus, to the Forum that lay before us in a glittering dusty haze, I swore a solemn oath to myself that I would never leave Rome again. That was when Fate should have shown me its second face, sent me a sign, a vision of the other entry of Honorius yesterday, fourteen years later: the same route but less well maintained, the same Emperor, but more faded, more nervous; the same temples, but fallen further into decay, boarded-up, overgrown with weeds; the same monuments, but despoiled, in the interim, of their gold and ornaments by the Goths; and I on the sidelines, on a shady slope under the pine trees, in rags, grey-haired, silent and motionless among the dutifully applauding people.

At that earlier time, Honorius rode in his gilded triumphal chariot, at his side in the seat of honor his father-in-law Stilicho, whom he invited again and again, with stately gestures, to share in the homage. He could hardly do otherwise, since it was Stilicho whom he had to thank for his Imperial glory, and for more than that. At that time there were no ominous cries – or perhaps we simply did not hear them through the cheers, the chanting of the priests in the forefront of the procession and the fanfares of the Germans who were taking up the rear. The secret envy which Honorius must, since his childhood, have felt toward this man who had acted as his guardian and who in fact was the invisible ruler of the Empire, kept festering within him. He controlled himself just as, for his part, Stilicho disguised his contempt and antipathy for his Imperial son-in-law. Those in the know waited — without discussing it openly — for the moment when the silent skirmishing would erupt into a deadly battle. I knew about this too, just as I knew — or thought I knew — everything in those days.

While the rose petals rained upon Honorius's procession — and thus upon me — I thought about how I could honor Stilicho in words without offending the Emperor, or how I could flatter the Emperor without neglecting to give Stilicho the full credit that was his due. Looking back, I don't know if I should laugh or cry over such short-sighted craftiness. Yesterday, as a spectator at Honorius's *second* entry, I saw my former self pass before my eyes, a famous man on his way to higher honors. My fall was imminent and I, who understood — or thought I understood — so much, didn't even suspect it.

I couldn't get rid of the cry *"Munera! Munera!"* which seemed to burst from the depths of the earth. As soon as the procession faded from view and the cordon was abandoned, the crowd began to disperse. There was no question of enthusiasm, but only an apathetic willingness to watch whatever chanced to come into view. It struck me that no one talked about the incident. On the contrary, I had the impression that the people who, like me, had stood on the shoulder of the road, and farther back, under the pine trees near the temple walls, avoided remaining to talk in groups.

I did not believe that those cries were coming from provocateurs. However, I waited a moment by the side of the road to see whether servants of the Prefect or other guards would appear from behind the temple buildings. But the place seemed filled exclusively with passersby, people who were walking back to the Forum and those — considerably in the minority, I might add — who wanted to try and catch something of the ceremonies in front of the heavily guarded Senate building.

Someone gave me alms, a woman, undoubtedly a Christian, one of the pious do-gooders who, in the hope of heavenly salvation, spend their days distributing money to the poor, even to those who don't hold out their hands. I went to sit in the dry grass with my back against the temple wall.

Over two decades I have seen a world perish, and

the birth of something new that is completely alien to me. In the district where I have lived since my official disappearance, in the ramshackle tenements or in one of the markets and squares in the neighborhood, I can still imagine that everything is the same as it was twenty years ago. Under the stinking landing of the tenement, among the stalls and the workshops and in the public baths, the chatter and jokes deal with the kinds of things that don't change quickly, and events take on the color of average humanity.

The climate in which the new ruling class lives is determined by questions of politics and religion. Leaning against the wall which cuts off access to the temples — most of them are in ruins — I saw men and women of that class passing in their palanquins, coiffed and clad in the style of the Eastern Empire which Honorius favors and which therefore the bishops don't dare to criticize. Creatures from another world, officials and merchants who have risen swiftly and become rich through dealings and negotiations with the Goths and call themselves *clarrissimi* and *nobilissimi* — and know quite well how to reconcile their Christianity with worldly activities. On this point, the Church gives them its blessings because without servants the Empire can't keep up its labyrinthine apparatus and today anyone who doesn't profess the Catholic faith isn't considered for any important post or office.

For the true believers — those who in an earlier day set the Christian tone here; idealists, living in strict observance of their doctrine of repentance and abjuration of the world, ready to let themselves be thrown to wild beasts for the sake of their convictions — I have always felt a certain respect. But today's newly powerful people — or those who would like to become powerful — those who have themselves baptized to serve their ambition or those who come from Christian families and have perfected the art of not letting the left hand know what the right hand is doing — these punish and exclude others with the same callous narrow-mindedness as those who persecuted Christians in the past and always with their own elect status on their lips — and they fill me with amazement and abhorrence.

Seven years ago I should still have laughed at the hypocrisy and pretentiousness of certain people, despite the fact that I was already their victim. But my worldly amusement turned to horror on the day that I heard that our exalted Emperor Honorius had

had his first advisor and right hand, the Defender of the Empire, the last sentinel between Rome and the barbarians, his father-in-law Stilicho, killed like a dog on the steps of the Christian altar in the basilica of Ravenna. Did the bishops protest? Did a cry of horror go up from the pious who are always pointing out, with great righteous indignation, the abuses that go on in Constantinople? The blood was mopped up, the Senate took on the difficult task of justifying the accusation that Stilicho was a traitor and then went on with the business of the day: a new murder, for complete security – the murder of Stilicho's only son.

With my back against the warm wall, I sat watching the crowded road and the people walking among the monuments and buildings which have not been declared contaminated because of their so-called heathen past.

Munera! Munera! Chills have often run down my spine when, during a gladiatorial contest, an unnatural dead silence fell over the arena just before the fatal stroke was given. A crowd of ten thousand held their breath and craned their necks while the final blood-stain seeped over the soiled, scuffed sand. Fear and lust, older than our oldest memories, hovered over

the amphitheatre. Another sacrifice — again, a toll
was paid to the powers of darkness which shall be
nameless. . . That's all, there is nothing more to be
said. The authorities have forbidden bloodshed as a
form of popular amusement, but their faith promises
salvation through continual inner contemplation of
the blood and suffering of a genuine victim.

I ask myself sometimes what impels most Christians to practice their religion: is it the belief that all
souls are equal before God, which was preached by
their solitary prophet? Or is it the turbid attraction
of martyrdom? No one living can remember it — it
is now many generations, more than one hundred
years, since the last Christians were put to death for
their convictions — but those of us who, before
Honorius issued his prohibition, had been accustomed to visit the games, knew from our own
experience the tense atmosphere of agony and thirst
for blood in which, for a brief moment, there was
communion between those who were going to die
and those who were going to watch them die. The
Christian dignitaries of the court who, on Honorius's orders, had butchered Stilicho while he clung
to the altar of the crucified one (so I have been told)
did not execute the sentence coldly and imperson-

ally; they did not satiate, like madmen, a need for vengeance – but voluptuously offered up a forbidden sacrifice.

I sat on the scorched grass in the heat of the sun and thought about these things: when I closed my eyes, I saw once more a horrible image that I knew not just from hearsay, as I did the death of Stilicho, but which I had seen with my own eyes: the hacked-off head of his wife Serena – my proud friend – stuck up on the City walls to frighten and discourage the Gothic besiegers. Every year in the days of the ancient republic, the head of a sacrificial horse was hung on the wall to ward off disaster. Serena's executioners did not know what they were doing, even though they tried to justify their senselessly cruel deed to the people by having their reasons shouted from the housetops. Under the ramparts of the Aurelian wall, the soldiers kept watch near the unrecognizably stained face with its open mouth and glassy eyes; her hair was still partially braided and full of clotted blood.

I saw it from where I stood among the people who were flocking there. Was this intended as a challenge, a declaration of independence to the barbarians, this woman's face which some of their com-

manders might perhaps remember from the time
when Stilicho negotiated with them? The head of a
Medusa, the blind and stiff figurehead of a Rome
which had changed irrevocably? The pitiful stinking
remains of a victim sacrificed in a moment of panic
to the powers of destruction?

I heard footsteps behind the wall. There was some
movement in the mass of ivy a few feet from where
I sat; there appeared to be an opening in the wall
there. Two men appeared among the vines — three
actually, because the first was carrying a dwarf on
his back: a nightmare figure came toward me — two
heads surmounting a gaudily dressed body, almost
cheek against cheek, one with soft features and a
carefully curled black fringe of beard, the other
convex, pock-marked. Behind them came a big burly
fellow who had to force himself through the opening. The vines crackled, there was a rain of leaves
and dust.

I remained sitting quietly where I was, a motionless spectator, undisturbed even when the other
threatened to stumble over my feet.

"Watch where you're going," I said to the double-
headed figure, who regained his balance with a

quick, elastic sideways leap.

"I don't need you to tell me what I should do. I know what I'm doing."

"Then you know too that it's strictly forbidden to circulate among the temple buildings?"

The man with the beard squinted; the pockmarked one gave a loud, throaty laugh. I pointed to the passersby in the road. "You'd sing another tune if there were *vigiles* in the neighborhood."

"You're wrong there. We're like one of the family with the authorities." (This time the pockmarked one, the dwarf.)

"Shut up! Let's go," said the big fellow who was taking up the rear.

The suspicion that I was dealing with the provocateurs compelled me to probe further. Why wasn't I more sensible? I didn't think about the ugly mugs of the police spies I had seen coming and going in the halls of the prefecture and in the prisons, that trash which would make false statements for money; who had apparently followed me and spied on me for a year, as I discovered too late. I seized the fat man by a fold of his tunic.

"You cried '*Munera!*' when the Emperor was going by."

The man stood with his shoulders hunched.

"And what if I did?"

"Why did you do it?"

"If you don't like it, you can take a good punch."

He pushed up his sleeve, slowly raised his arm and clenched his fist. I pointed to his bulging, ropey muscles.

"And you used to fight in the arena."

"That's none of your business." (But I could tell that he was flattered.)

"*I* called out," said the dwarf, who had slid down from his companion's back. He put his hands to his mouth and brought forth a hollow, echoing sound, muffled now, but unmistakably the same as that which had just thrown the procession into confusion.

"Were you paid to do that?"

"No, it's our hobby," said the dwarf. The three of them burst into laughter.

The man with the beard squatted down next to me and looked at me with yellow cat's eyes. "You ask too many questions. Who and what are you?"

He waited, peering at me, smiling with parted lips which were too red, too moist. I found him more repulsive than the freak or the obese muscle man.

"I am a person of independent means," I said. "I'm a passerby in Rome, a spectator. At the moment I'm sitting here to avoid the crowd."

The dwarf made lightning-quick grabbing motions. "Oh, yes, I can imagine how you've handled things — or rather how you've taken hold of one thing and another. Are you too a victim of the new laws?"

"Me too?" I had learned that it was better not to understand every insinuation immediately.

"We've been out of work since the decrees outlawing the games," said the man with the beard, still smiling. "That one there is good for nothing now that there's no more combat."

Suddenly I recognized him: the blue-black beard that seemed painted on his chin and cheeks; his boneless body, his light eyes which looked like the agate or topaz eyes which in the past artists had given to images of the gods.

"Pylades the mime! I've seen you as Bacchus. But that was more than ten years ago. What are you doing now?"

"Ah, ah, Dionysus is not dead," said the dwarf, who moved close to his friends and nuzzled between them like an affectionate lapdog.

"That probably means that you operate a bordello."

"Then should we say that we're out of work?" giggled the dwarf.

They were getting on my nerves; I wanted to leave them. I stood up. "I salute you."

Before I had taken three steps, the dwarf had grabbed a piece of my clothing.

"We've misjudged you. You're not one of those who have long fingers. Here's your capital back that you get your income from."

He held out to me on his palm the coin (pinched by him in the interim) that the charitable lady had given to me.

"I see that I can still learn something from you," I said.

"It would really be a pity if we didn't become better acquainted now," said Pylades, while he walked down the slope next to me. "We must have a talk."

"I didn't know that we shared common interests."

"Oh but yes! The good old times."

He snapped his fingers over his shoulder, a signal for the others to follow us. We were standing on the pavement now, among the strolling passersby. I wanted to turn in the direction of the Subura, but

Pylades put his hand on my arm.

"May I offer you a beaker of wine on the other side, in Apicius's tavern?"

At that moment I should have refused curtly and gone on my way. He filled me with aversion and resentment and uneasiness at the same time, because he had awakened my curiosity. There had to be a connection between his sudden appearance, the cry of "*Munera! Munera!*" and the second entry of Honorius. Yesterday something came within my reach; I don't know what it is, or whether I should welcome it. There are changes in the air; now the signs must be interpreted.

In the past, when I was in Honorius's retinue, I was present day in and day out at the spectacles offered by the City to the Emperor in honor of his first formal entry. The performance of this same Pylades, who had the privilege of being the third in a series of illustrious holders of that name, was heralded as a high point of the festivities. And that would certainly have been the case if the passions which it provoked had not unleashed a commotion far more memorable than the spectacle itself.

After a wild ballet of bacchantes and satyrs in an exceptionally sumptuous setting (it was, under the

circumstances, an insane waste of money), Pylades
sprang from a litter of interlaced vines: the god of
wine, naked except for a loincloth of panther skin
and crowned with clusters of grapes.

From a distance he seemed, even more than he did
today, to be a youth, an ageless creature; his body
quivered like a young tree in the wind; when he
moved in a certain way, the gleam that ran over his
skin suggested the play of sunlight on water, or light
splashing on wind-tossed leaves. He leaped like a
deer, stalked like a beast of prey or whirled and
swayed in dances which were more sensual and
shameless than those of Syrian harlots.

Confusion and disapproval could be read on the
faces of Honorius's courtiers, who had not been in
the habit, in Milan or Ravenna, of attending spectacles like this. The situation grew worse when the
bacchantes rushed forth en masse onto the stage,
stamping their feet and, after having surrendered
themselves to lewd games with the god, began to tear
at him in a frenzy.

The manner in which Pylades mimed the martyr's
death was incomparable: shaken by voluptuous
spasms, while blood from artfully concealed hogs'
bladders streamed over his face and limbs,he fell all

at once into what was finally no more than a shapeless heap of debris. The public on the highest benches roared with enthusiasm; a rustling and murmuring of continual excitement went through the rows of patricians in the lower seats. There were glances at the platform where Honorius sat with his court.

The Emperor was visibly impressed (the eunuchs in Constantinople who had raised him and his brother had spent much time on the formation of his aesthetic tastes, a circumstance from which I too enjoyed the benefits); many of the courtiers and high officials sat with set faces, but naturally no one had the courage to show his displeasure by leaving.

The next number on the program was a gladiatorial combat, trident and casting-net against sword and shield — one of the mass exhibitions in which twenty or thirty pairs were in the arena at the same time, and the victors immediately competed against each other until finally only one of them survived. The spectators, still fired up from Pylades' performance, cheered on the combatants, shrieking for blood. When the first victims had fallen, the crowd could not contain itself; even the Emperor clutched the balustrade tightly. All around him and his retinue, who knew how to preserve decorum, tens of thousands bellowed and howled, sweeping themselves into an emotional maelstrom.

Suddenly it was noticed that someone was standing in the arena who did not belong there. It took a few minutes before the gladiators became aware of this intrusive presence and began to hesitate. Some of them let their weapons fall, the net-throwers withdrew to a safe distance. The roaring in the stands diminished. The intruder moved about in the middle of the sand, waving his arms, exhorting the combatants in a voice breaking with emotion. He wore a habit, he was sunburned and unkempt like a hermit come from the desert. Fragments of his argument came through to where I sat; he could not be understood in the higher stands, where people were becoming restless again, the ill-natured restlessness caused by interrupted tension, which quickly reached its boiling point and inevitably erupted into threats and violence.

"Go on! Fight!" screamed the *nobilissimi* in the first rows, while the man below, his arms raised, attempted to drive the gladiators from the arena with a torrent of words. Trainers and overseers came running from all sides, but they could not silence the monk whom they dared not seize, nor move the irresolute, waiting gladiators to fight again.

Courtiers of various factions crowded about the Emperor, arguing and disputing with one another at the tops of their voices. I could not see Honorius himself, but I had a clear view of the man who bent over him, talking and gesturing fiercely with his long, pale hands: the poet Prudentius, a recent convert to Christianity, bursting with religious zeal and ambition. Everyone knew that the Emperor was not particularly fond of the man and his work, but he did not have the courage to keep him at a distance because Prudentius was a protégé of the bishops.

Stilicho and Serena were sitting on the marble seats behind Honorius. As Prudentius pleaded more and more vehemently for the immediate cessation of the performance, attention in the Imperial company was fastened sharply on Stilicho. Every now and then I caught a glimpse of him through the milling courtiers: erect, motionless, self-controlled, he waited to be brought into this affair; but something in the way he held his head and in the tense line of his neck and shoulders (I was familiar with his reactions) betrayed his complete -- although vigilant -- absorption in deciding his strategy.

Serena leaned toward him, but they did not speak to each other. She too was vigilant, listening without showing any emotion, but I could see the jewels of her earrings sparkling against her apparently immobile cheek. This time Stilicho made a mistake: in evaluating the situation, he had not taken into account the passions aroused by Pylades' performance. What he expected — that the Emperor would finally turn to him as usual to resolve the crisis, giving him the opportunity to present Prudentius's proposal in his own somewhat modified, more diplomatic form — would surely have happened under other circumstances, but then it was too late.

I didn't believe that Stilicho really grasped what was going on among the eddying mob in the stands. It was one of those instances which I myself had experienced repeatedly in the past — where the intrinsic difference became perceptible between his nature and that of the native-born Romans. He did not realize what was clear to Prudentius — that the monk must, for his own protection, be made to vanish somehow from the arena and that the only way to accomplish that was to call off the gladiatorial contest. Stilicho had no instinct for the cloudy or ambiguous — that was later to be his undoing. Looking back on that day ten years ago in the Colosseum, I now believe that that was the turning-point of Stilicho's career and destiny, and that it was an event which had an equally decisive effect upon my life.

I remember how I stood up along with the multitude when somewhere from out of the highest galleries a demented horde came pouring down the stairs and over the balustrades and railings, to throw themselves into the arena. To my knowledge it had never happened before that the spectators had actually intervened when something went on in the arena that wasn't to their taste. It was this fact — that the situation was unprecedented, completely unexpected — that made it so terrifying.

The gladiators and overseers drew back behind the barriers which normally served to protect the public from escaped wild animals. It was only much later that soldiers from the Emperor's retinue succeeded in dispelling the raging mob, which could not stop kicking the mutilated corpse through the arena. The theatre emptied amidst indescribable confusion. White as chalk, leaning on his bishops, Honorius tottered from his loge. On that same day, he issued the order to ban the games permanently, and proclaimed the unfortunate victim to be a martyr.

As I accompanied Pylades through the streets behind the Aemilia basilica, it occurred to me that I was walking next to my tangible destiny. I found his mincing gait annoying along with the coquettish way in which from time to time he shrugged his mantle more closely about him. Before he turned corners, he slackened his pace and gestured invitingly to me as if he were a host leading a tour of his property. He didn't speak to me; the bustle in the street forced us to step aside continually, separating us for some distance. When I looked back I saw the gladiator and the dwarf in our wake.

I knew now what memories, repressed for more than twenty years, determined my attitude toward Pylades. Something about his appearance, his glance, his movements, above all his aura of theatrical make-believe, his capacity for ambiguity, the embodiment of perversity, called up things which I had wanted to forget: old doubts and shame, my life in Alexandria under the roof of my benefactor, Olympiodorus. When I let Pylades lure me to that tavern, I still did not know exactly who or what he reminded me of, but at every step my reluctance grew. I needed to shake off my uneasiness the way a horse ripples its flanks to drive away stinging flies.

I stopped him on the threshold of Apicius's public house.

"I used to admire your artistry, but that's no reason for us to go drinking together."

"What are you really afraid of?" he asked over his shoulder.

Although the time for the midday meal had already passed, there were still many people eating in the tavern, a natural result of the large turnout for Honorius's entry. I knew the cellar by reputation; the proprietor had a bad name. The place was murky, like a cave. Reddish smoke hung in the rear, above a row of portable charcoal cookers. I pushed my way to sit facing Pylades at a free corner of one of the tables. The dwarf and the fat man looked for other places. I found it difficult to eat the pieces of meat and fish without bolting them down; I controlled myself mostly because Pylades did not take his eyes off me.

"I still don't understand why I am being honored," I said, drinking to him.

"I can see immediately . . . whether someone belongs with us."

Carefully, he licked his lips, like a great cat.

I contemplated my beaker without answering.

"Listen, don't act as if you don't understand. You're one of us, you hold the old beliefs, in *Liber Pater*, surely, at the least, in the god who gives himself freely and joyously . . ."

As he spoke these words, he shoved his beaker against mine so that the wine spattered over the table. Although nothing around us appeared to change, the noise seemed to lessen as if there were secret listeners, as if we were being stealthily watched.

I lifted my beaker and drank.

"Bacchus will never again be more to me than this," I said, "but that's not negligible when it's a question of a decent wine."

"Everyone here is a good sort." Pylades was becoming impatient. "You don't have to try to evade the issue."

"I don't equivocate. I say what I mean."

"But you're not of . . . this," he said. He dipped a finger in the wine and traced a cross on the table top.

I shook my head.

"So, what then?" he insisted, suddenly angry.

"Isis? Mithras? The Syrian gods? Say it! Are you a coward?"

"I'm nothing," I said, shrugging.

"A philosopher?"

"I feel flattered."

"And the death then, the resurrection, immortality?"

"I don't know anything about it."

Now his face became a mask of resentment; his eyes glittered with hostility.

"I curse your sort, that pride, that superior little smile. They have no need for mysteries, oh no! A rational explanation for every secret, and what cannot be explained does not exist. You go through life deaf and blind. You don't even realize what you're missing."

"Save yourself the trouble. The secrets and riddles of the so-called commonplace are enough for me — and, by the way, I have no desire to solve all of them, even if I were to be granted the ability to do it —"

Pylades tried another tack.

"I haven't asked your name. Something tells me that in your case it's not very important to know what you're usually called. But you can't fool me, even though you walk around in rags. You're an educated man, you belong to a distinguished house. I have eyes and ears for things like that."

I shrugged. "It's unimportant, my friend."

"Do you think so?"

I didn't like his look — appraising, sly, full of secret satisfaction . . . a desire to run away came over me: to slip sideways from the bench like a crab, to vanish far from Pylades into the labyrinth of my distant quarter and so to my safe corner in the insula Iulia. But with the man's infallible seventh sense, he read my intention; before I could move, he put his hand on my arm.

"One word, one gesture from me, and you disappear, quickly and quietly, into the sewer — an intruder who denies the existence of the mysteries, perhaps a potential spy for the authorities . . ."

"What do you really want from me? In the district where I live, they sometimes call me *Pro Se* because I never meddle in other people's affairs. I'm just a seedy clerk. Years before the Gothic invasion, I lost my post and my connections. Now and then I earn a little money giving lessons and writing letters and petitions. That's all there is to know about me."

Pylades fingered my threadbare toga and shook his head, smiling.

"You meddle with nothing and no one. But that didn't prevent your pointing out to my friends and me that we had committed a minor infraction of the law, did it? You would have done better not to have seen us when we came through the wall."

I could have replied that they had left the forbidden ground and emerged into public view in a manner that was not especially discreet, and that, moreover, they had made themselves extremely noticeable by stumbling over my legs. If the cry 'Munera! Munera!' had not disturbed Honorius's entry, I wouldn't have paid any attention to someone creeping through the temple wall.

I wanted to leave. For a moment Pylades had captured my interest; I was caught up by the memory of what he had been — and of course what I had been. But more than that — something about him made him seem to be a thread in the pattern of my life, an element in the network of my secret self. I felt that we had nothing to say to each other; I did not want any further contact with him. I thought that, in order to grasp the significance of this fleeting encounter on that particular day, I did not need him and his one and a half followers.

I know now whom he reminded me of — even though there was no physical resemblance: Olympiodorus's confidante, that slave from Syria or Persia, whose task it was to prepare the boys in the house for what would be expected of them there and to bring them to reason if they appeared reluctant. Like a dark silent Hermes Psychopompos, he conducted his master's favorites through the labyrinth of that house in Alexandria — those who should know say it deserved a place among the wonders of the world.

Black marble floors, pillars of porphyry and basalt; at every turn a view of adjacent enclosed gardens or the reflecting rectangle of a pool; and, alternatively, twilit rooms where one walked over soft panther skins and where there were the undefined odors of incense and spices. Statues of gods and athletes populated the galleries — frozen perfection.

The only female attributes one could admire in that house were the breasts of the sphinxes and harpies who stood, life-sized, on either side of all the doorways; and, in miniature, as decorative motifs on furniture and utensils. Endlessly repeated on murals, always before one's eyes wherever one was, whatever one did, were female monsters with wings, claws and scaly tails. The masculine statues in marble — even an Antinous, a Narcissus — nearly androgynous, were incarnations of the daylight world of harmony and light, while the dream creatures with the breasts were preposterous, impossible apparitions which belonged to the troubled secrets of the night, experiences of lust and pain.

Olympiodorus sent his proteges to the best schools and tutors in Alexandria, to make them, in conformance with the Greek ideal of knowledge and beauty, into young philosophers and athletes — but he expected from them, between sunset and dawn, compliance in alien rituals invented by his slave.

I pulled my mantle from Pylades' fingers. But of course I remained seated. The hour passed when I usually sought my habitual corner in the public baths where I acted as oracle to my unlettered neighbors. Slightly drunk, filled with aversion for myself, for Pylades and for the low den in which we found ourselves, I thought with the melancholy of one who had gone astray, about my bench in the *tepidarium*; about the shopkeeper of the district whom I promised to help take stock of his wares; about the inhabitants of the *insula* Cornelia for whom I was to draw up a letter of protest to their landlord; about all the acquaintances who were now there, leaning against the steamy tile walls.

Pylades tried again to intimidate me in various ways — a little game which could deceive no one and whose only purpose could be to find out where I was vulnerable. I did not rise to the bait. I didn't understand, for that matter, where he was trying to lead me. His hints and questions bored me. I kept drinking, picturing to myself how, at that moment, in the hastily restored and cleaned galleries of the Palatine, Honorius was playing the little emperor as usual, waving his heavily beringed hand condescendingly, his toga, resplendent with sparkling embroidery, artfully draped to conceal his meagre, childish body. They say that, despite the bishops' opposition, he had increased his demands for ceremonies like those which are practiced in Constantinople.

In those days during my recitations, I often had to stand by his side; to him I was no more than a verse-making, verse-reciting instrument which he could command with a gesture to begin and to cease. It was reported that he valued my work highly, but he never spoke to me; he looked at me without seeing me. But

I got a good look at him: his hair, plastered in symmetrical curls against his skull, his haughty, yellowish profile. To learn how he should react, he threw frequent quick glances at Stilicho, who knew, always, how to preserve the perfect balance — sometimes giving a nod of approval accompanied by a slight ironic smile to minimize my lyric flight without criticizing the meaning or the cadence; sometimes giving greater importance to the actual impact of a verse by a barely perceptible change of expression.

I never believed that Stilicho had any real literary insight and taste, but he, more than anyone, gave me the opportunity to develop my talents in that area (and he, more than anyone, profited from it). Usually, during my recitations, he stood next to the Emperor — where, by the way, he belonged because of his rank and prominence — but not too close: at a deliberately proper distance, just outside the carpet spread around the Imperial throne, on the marble which shone like a mirror.

An irony of fate that I, who on these occasions had, through rhetorical artifice, greatly exaggerated the outrages of Honorius's enemies, had to remain silent after the murder in Ravenna; that I, who denounced the hypocrisy of Gildo (he poisoned his adversaries while they sat as guests at his table), had no words to describe the Emperor's treachery; that I, who once wrote a poem in which the villain Rufinus was charged in the underworld with his crimes by the ghosts of his victims, could not open my mouth to accuse, in the names of Stilicho and Serena, the man who is carried now in great pomp in his palanquin through Rome, Master of the Empire of the Occident, ally and friend of – and yes, relation in marriage to – the Goths who six years earlier had played havoc here, burning and plundering everything in their path.

"It's an old geezer," said a woman's voice above my head. The dwarf and the ex-fighter appeared from the ruddy depths of the public house, accompanied by a slattern, who now stood leaning against the table. Long strings of henna-dyed hair, escaping from a slovenly bun, straggled over her shoulders; a scent of cheap perfume and bath oil rose from the folds of her garments.

"Push off, Urbanilla," Pylades said irritably. "Nobody asked you to come here."

"Oh, yes, *they* did." The girl jerked a shoulder

toward Pylades' confederates.

The dwarf clambered onto the bench next to Pylades. In order to deceive what had once more become the two-headed monster, I pretended to be drunk and mumbled something into my beaker. That roused the dwarf's contempt. "He really will not do," he said.

"I don't know yet what to think of him."

"Don't waste your time. You can see, can't you, that he's worthless. You can get another one."

"Oh yes, that's so simple," Pylades said sarcastically. "Just leave that to me. I don't make mistakes."

I judged that the moment had come to get up from my seat, bawling unintelligibly. The fat man made a move in my direction, but Pylades restrained him. I shuffled past the girl, who spat a couple of insults at me — boozer, filthy swine. I really did not expect them to let me go. Halfway down the street, I pretended to stumble over a peddler's baskets, in order to look behind me. The three of them had left the tavern. At first they began to follow me, but when they realized that I was wandering aimlessly, they joined me. In the hope of getting rid of them, I chose the ever-crowded streets and alleys near the Forum. But they had attached themselves to me

like leeches, determined to find out where I lived. I
was reminded of how I used to walk in these same
squares and steps, at propitious times of the day,
always surrounded by my clients. I burst into
laughter. The ex-gladiator poked me; Pylades ob-
served with contempt that I could not hold my
liquor.

"Don't start with him," the dwarf said again. For
the umpteenth time, they began to quarrel. They
discussed my appearance, my demeanor: according
to Pylades, if I were properly dressed and shaved,
and after a brief period of retraining in social
practices — which they believed I had clearly forgotten — I could be very useful. The dwarf doubted
that and attempted with a vehemence which I
attributed to jealousy, to persuade Pylades to abandon me to my fate.

"Who's in charge here, you or me?" Pylades asked
coldly.

I could still only guess at the nature of their
intentions toward me. They certainly found it
worth their while not to let me out of their sight. It
had been going on too long: I was as sober again as
I had been in the morning, and I was annoyed with
this unwanted company.

2.

Like a ghost surrounded by malignant spectres in a borderland of death, I wandered through the Imperial heart of the City which had for years seemed more unreal to me each time I came here. It was still broad daylight, but the sun was in the west; the columns threw elongated shadows across the porticos. That is the hour when the new Rome — or the non-Rome; I don't know what to call it — takes on a dangerous formlessness; the crowd consists no longer of separate individuals with recognizable faces and gestures, but becomes a buzzing stream of spilled colors moving between the buildings which seem, in the honeyed light, to be made of eggshells, about to crack. One has the feeling that with a wave of the hand, one could sweep away the image of reality like a glossy film, behind which lies chaos, darkness.

Some choose to believe that it was the Gothic occupation which irrevocably changed the character of Rome within a generation. I myself often tried to explain away my feeling of alienation by attributing it to my advancing age, and to the complete reversal of my fate ten years ago. But I know that none of this is true: the Goths are not responsible for this metamorphosis; the natural deterioration of age has nothing to do with my condition, nor do the events which so radically transformed my life. These things are the culmination of a process which began twenty years ago when I left Alexandria to come to Rome.

I could have recognized the signs if I had chosen to. The Rome that I loved, that I venerated, no longer existed, had not existed for a long time . . . if indeed it had ever existed at all. Perhaps it existed only in the dreams of an Egyptian with a Greek education who had, under the colonnades and in the study halls of Alexandria, formed an idealized image of the civilization of his time. It seemed to me that this lustre was reflected in people like Ammanianus Marcellinus, Praetextatus Symmachus, Rutilius Namatianus, Serena. But they too lived in a different world from that whose demeanor and style they adopted. When I think of them, I remember uncertainties, contradictions, which had not struck me at the time, or which I may well have noticed but refused to accept. In the course of those years, I had become increasingly aware of the uneasiness that clouded Stilicho's life and aspirations, despite his resolute commitment to Rome.

He knew that what he wanted to accomplish was justified, and he knew too that he would never be able to attain those goals — not because he was deficient in any way, nor because others worked against his projects (although this was certainly the case, more even than he ever suspected), but because his strength of purpose and abilities and those of his partisans were no match for the indefinable but clearly perceptible pressure from without as well as within: a torrent of change. Stilicho had the courage to combat the incomprehensible with untiring tenacity and he was an excellent strategist who knew how to change his tactics as often as he thought necessary. But he must have known that his enemies would take advantage of that very fact, because it could make him seem unpredictable, or even untrustworthy. The consequent erosion affected us all.

I see images from that former life as though they appear on a mural partially obliterated by age: a face, a gesture, the outline of a figure, a group, in faded colors, suggesting what it was when it was fresh, but now eaten by decay, cracked, slowly peeling. Yesterday, as I wandered through the crowded streets between the government buildings with those three at my heels like warders, I was assaulted anew — as

I had been so often in the past — by the realization
that my old friends were dead and gone. I could
touch the railings, the columns where their hands
had rested; I recognized at every step a place which
I had passed in my walks with them.

Despite some open spaces left here and there by
fires, the overall picture of this sea of houses remains
roughly unchanged, and I recognized the spot where,
strolling and chatting, dazzled each time anew by the
splendor of the spectacle, I used to point out to my
companions the play of light and shadow over the
aqueduct. Pylades' mantle fluttering before my eyes;
the dwarf — that strange gnome — now in front of me,
then again behind me; the fat man's fist planted
annoyingly in my back. . . all of it, even the most
concrete — walls and trees, the people I brushed
against and whose breath touched me as I passed
them — all seemed unreal to me. Sometimes in
earlier days I had seen columns of white or ochre
dust rising here and, squinting against the glare, I
had imagined that this was a procession of spectres
filing through the living crowd. Now I myself was
one of those ghosts.

On all sides of us were tall, white shapes; we were
in the Forum of Trajan, a place which for years I had

avoided like the plague. There they were: the twice dead, with their bloated marble faces, in their marble togas, petrified in an oratorical pose, heroically brandishing the staff of command or the book scroll. I was seized by rage against this grotesque and impotent pack of immortals. Many of these, since the invasion of the Goths, were headless, armless. Some of them had been knocked off their pedestals and lay awaiting restoration. I can find my way among those heroes and masters. A sudden desire to torment myself impelled me to hurry to a pedestal to look at a face that no longer resembled anyone, to read an inscription that I knew by heart.

"The Goths forgot you," I told the statue, surprising myself because I did not speak only to make my role as a drunkard more credible.

I noticed that some pieces of the pedestal were missing. Before long, no one will be able to read respectfully how, fifteen years ago, the august, blessed and deeply learned Emperors Hadrian and Arcadius had ordered the erection of this white marble doll.

"Not even life-sized; no gold or bronze set in," said the dwarf, appraising it with contempt. "No inlaid eyes either — the barbarians must have stolen them. . ."

I pointed to the head with the laurel wreath. "Ah no, you were already blind. . . Smaller than a real man. . . Everything tasteful and elegant, but on a reduced scale. . . Little poet, little orator, little eulogist. . . ."

Pylades, who had been waiting peevishly, turned and snapped at us, "How long is this going to go on? I'm not going to stay here forever!"

"He's talking rubbish to that statue."

"Balcho, grab him under the arms, carry him for all I care, but let's go!"

"Where to?" The ex-fighter did not dare to contradict Pylades, but he had had enough; for some time he had been silently steaming with rage.

The dwarf saw a chance to get rid of me. "Leave him here. He doesn't do you any good."

Pylades' face became taut with anger.

I clung for security to the marble folds full of dust and dead insects and went on with my monologue — primarily out of a desire for self-preservation, but also for the sheer pleasure of thinking out loud.

"Tribune and notary. . . jewel of letters. . . inspired by the spirit of Homer and the muse of Vergil. . . It can be nothing less."

"He's dead drunk!" cried the dwarf, immediately

assuming the role of agitator, leering at Pylades.

The fat man, who had been standing behind me for some time, irresolute and exasperated, now stooped down, jerked loose a chunk of a cracked paving stone and hurled it with full force at the marble face, smashing it to pieces. "Now you won the argument," he said to me. "He won't irritate you any more."

The crowd appeared to have been waiting for a signal of this kind: all sorts of trash — clumps of mud, half-eaten fruit — came flying through the air. People were running toward us from all sides, eager to see what was going on. There were those, too, who began to shout for the *vigiles.* A swirl of excitement from the vicinity of the arcades announced the approach of the guardians of public order. However, when Pylades, with the dwarf on his back, bolted through a path in the mob cleared by the ex-fighter, not one of the shouters and pointers made any attempt to stop them. I was just able to catch a glimpse of the dwarf's triumphant face bobbing above the crowd, before the trio disappeared from sight.

I had no time to rejoice over that: the next thing I knew, someone had seized me, crying, "He was there! He was part of it!" I was pushed and jostled toward the *vigiles*. At this point, a diversion occurred around the palanquin. Its occupant pushed the curtain aside and leaned out. "Stop! It's a mistake! Let that man go!"

Now that the palanquin had emerged from the crush, I recognized the signs of a grand style: bearers and attendants soberly clad in the old manner — no finery, no colors, the man in the palanquin sitting erect, one hand motionless on the white folds at his shoulder.

"A flagrant case of vandalism," began one of the guards.

"That's certainly not true. He belongs to my retinue; he's one of my clients."

"There are witnesses. We bear the responsibility. By order of the Prefect, anyone who does damage like this—"

A hand swept sideways in a short, choppy movement. "The witnesses were mistaken. I will personally vouch for him. I know the Prefect. I am Marcus Anicius Rufus."

Reluctantly, the *vigiles* let me go.

3.

In the house of Marcus Anicius Rufus, the lamps were already lighted. At the direction of a slave, I went to sit on a bench in one of the rooms bordering the atrium. In the distance was a garden. I could smell damp plants and earth; I heard the murmur of water streaming into the basin of an invisible fountain. Unlike so many others at present, Marcus Anicius Rufus had had the courage and good taste to refrain from having the murals – solely mythological scenes – covered with whitewash. I was absorbed in contemplation of the rape of Persephone (the center panel, which depicted the abduction of the girl by the dark god, was in the room where I sat) when he entered. I rose and thanked him for his help.

"The honor and the pleasure are entirely mine. I could see what was happening from my palanquin. It wasn't you who smashed that statue."

"I could have done it. I've often been inclined to do it. That statue is a failure in every way."

A slave brought wine. My host filled the goblets and offered one to me.

When we were alone again, he said suddenly, over the rim of his lifted cup, "I know who you are."

Resolved to say neither yes nor no, I held his gaze while we drank. He had changed somewhat in the twenty years since I had seen him last, in the house of his relatives who were my employers at the time. Sharp eyes he had, and a good memory. He smiled as he set down his goblet. "It's wise of you to say nothing. You can trust me."

"There's nothing between us. I didn't ask you for that favor which you so kindly bestowed on me. Under no circumstances do I want to take up your valuable time. Please have your slave show me out."

It was very quiet in the house for that time of day. I understood that he deliberately kept his family and servants at a distance. Someone had closed the wooden shutters which separated the atrium from the other rooms. When I had stepped over the threshold of the reception room, I was surrounded by Persephone's playmates, reddish and ocher-colored, fleeing in panic across the walls. Now I noticed the household altar in a corner.

"Do stay a while," he said from behind me. "Won't you make an offering to the memory of my nephews Olybrius and Probinus?"

"I don't practice that form of *pietas*." As I spoke, I realized how dim the memory of those dead men had become.

He walked past me and placed his hand on the stone dwelling of the *lares*. "Surely, like me, you honor the old gods?"

"I don't honor the gods."

For the first time he looked at me with a glimmer of suspicion. "But you're not a Christian?"

"I'm not a Christian."

"Stilicho was a Christian. I've asked myself how it was possible that you, with your views —"

"You don't know my views."

"I've read and reread your poems," he said sharply.

I moved away from him. As he stood there next to his domestic altar, a white-robed, dignified figure in the starkly simple room, I thought that twenty years ago he would have seemed to me a paragon of all manly Roman virtues, pillar of the state, *pater familias* and protector of the shades of his ancestors who crowded, invisible, behind him.

"I'm someone else," I said, less coldly now, because I pitied him. We stood facing each other; only the shallow basin of the *impluvium* was between us. It might just as well have been an abyss, or the impassable Styx. "I'm someone else. I don't write poems. I shouldn't want to."

Doubtful and perplexed, he threw up his hands. "Then what do you want? What's happened to you? What are you doing, what do you believe in?"

"I must go."

He blocked my way with a violent movement that reminded me suddenly of Olybrius; the thin flames trembled in the lamps. A long time ago, in rooms like these, with the same golden light glowing on painted columns hung with garlands, I had jested and drunk with those two youths who had been named consuls at an age when the less fortunate had to wear themselves out just to obtain a place as client in a "great" house.

Olybrius, dancing, adorned after the antique custom, and Probinus, who held his wine better than his brother, used to open sliding doors like these for me so that they could take me to their dinner guests. That large villa, which was later pillaged and burned by the Goths, was one of the most beautiful in Rome: a series of halls and galleries where a silence hung — never wholly dispelled even by the brothers' exuberance — that seemed to emanate from the unseen rooms of their mother Proba, the Christian. The odor of her piety seeped through every crack; while flute-players performed in the *tablinum*, she received priests in her own chambers. Every morning her confessor and her devout women friends had to work their way — small, unworldly processions — through the crowds of clients waiting for her sons.

"You're in trouble."

"No, not if you let go of my cloak."

"I can't believe my eyes and ears. Disgraced before Rome, before the people who used to be your friends. . . Condemned to be a living dead man, banished to the underworld . . ."

Was it the glow of the lamps, the ambience — for the first time in ten years an environment unlike the stinking tenement holes — was it the reminder of Olybrius and Probinus, was it the painted figures on the walls, which caused me to abandon my reserve, to yield to the temptation of being once more, for an instant, the man I once was? Through the open door, I could see, directly before me in the reception room, the dark form of Pluto, lord of the realm of shadows. I spoke aloud the proud, consoling words which long ago, in a poem, I had put into the mouth of the god — words addressed to the victim in his arms, who turns her face away from him:

> Don't believe that only darkness reigns.
> Another star is shining, another light,
> On another world, on other beings.

Marcus Anicius embraced me as if I were a long-lost relative.

"Allow me to help you. In my house you're completely safe."

"Nothing could be a greater threat to *your* safety than the presence of someone who, by judgment, has been denied fire and water."

I saw in his eyes and in the stubborn lines around his mouth that no words of mine could dissuade him. Blunt rejection, flight — no other course was open to me now. I cursed my momentary weakness. I told him once more that he was mistaken, that in contrast to those who were exiled to Hades, I was quite satisfied with my life. I did not have to beg or steal; I was able to make myself useful. I couldn't think of a greater freedom than mine.

He chose to ignore these arguments and continued to stare at me in baffled irritation. "You are accepting a life without human dignity."

"'Truly belonging to the human species means refusing to bow to the caprices of fate in essential matters.'"

"You're quoting Seneca. You know better than I that he rejects retirement, that he advises every man to serve the public interest to the best of his ability — how does he put it? — 'Render service to friends, family, fellow citizens . . .' For a man of your calibre to neglect his remarkable gifts — that seems to me to be the same as misusing them. Especially now, when it's more necessary than ever to defend the values and principles of our fathers. You're not deaf and blind! Surely you must have noticed that there are forces at work to transform radically the spirit of Rome! There are still enough people who are ready to do their utmost to prevent that and to keep alive the ideal of a balance between commonsense, a sense of duty and a great vision. We need you!"

A familiar theme. The young client of Olybrius and Probinus, fresh from Alexandria, trembled with emotion and eagerness when one of the powerful Anicii came up to him, gave him a friendly tap on the shoulder and, in the name of the patricians of Rome, commissioned him to write a panegyric celebrating the consulship of the two Anicii nephews.

He wanted nothing more, this freshly minted Roman, Claudius Claudianus; even before the other had finished speaking, verses began to buzz in the poet's head, a stream of words broke loose, uncontrollable as the Nile when it overflows its banks.

I did not stint on compliments in my address to these two newly appointed young consuls, my pupils, to whom I imparted the principles of rhetoric and a smattering of literary knowledge; nor did I disappoint the entire Roman aristocracy sitting behind them, who thought to ensure their future by paying this Imperial homage to the class of Senators. I praised their virtues to the skies; I supported their claim to the Emperor's favor with a torrent of arguments drawn from history and mythology. But the real object of my love and honor was Rome, City and Empire, legend and reality, a dazzling and sublime world of thoughts and actions which inspired my pen and later strengthened my voice at the ceremonial reading before the Senate. Rome, Goddess and Benefactress, Mother of laws whose reign gives us Heaven on Earth. . . .

A living dead man. That is what Marcus Anicius called me when I stood next to him in his atrium. He himself looked like a corpse, shut away in the twilight of the grave. It would take sorcery to bring back the dreams and deeds of vanished centuries. I did not know whether to laugh or weep at the sight of this upright man who was still living in the days of the Republic, consorting with the likes of Cato, Brutus and Cicero, piously tending his *lares* and *penates*.

"We need you!" For what? To dethrone Honorius, to expel the bishops? To defy the passion for salvation and the mystique of martyrdom and restore the sobriety and self-discipline which failed to inspire the Roman citizen four hundred years ago?

Looking at him, I was suddenly overcome by the bitter feeling that I might be partially responsible for his state of mind. Nothing can erase those words which I had written one day, black on white, merging the ideal image of the *Pax Romana* with the Roman thought which had inspired him and his peers:

> Rome is a mother, not a harsh mistress.
> To those who submit to her, she grants
> the right to call themselves her citizens.
> Through wisdom and love, she brings
> together the far corners of the earth.
> Thanks to the peace she keeps, every
> foreigner finds a fatherland. We travel

> without fear, we enjoy going to Thule,
> penetrating far-flung territories to drink
> from the Rhone or the Orontes. Rome
> alone has made one people from many
> peoples; she cherishes the vanquished
> at her breast and unites all mankind
> under one name.

Ringing words! Tears had come to my eyes when I delivered that panegyric at Stilicho's first consulate. I saw, I felt, the august presence of Mother Rome: over the heads of the audience of Senators and courtiers, behind the columns of the porticos, I could discern the sea of marble, the City that was her crown, and beyond that white radiance, the Alban mountains far off in a haze of heat.

Since those days, I have taken another look at our goddess and benefactress. At times she seems like a dead queen, lying in state, emitting a stench of decomposition which penetrates even the balm and bandages enwrapping her, crawling with maggots under her jewels; at other times, like an old brothelkeeper, withered and bedizened, who receives the worst scoundrels and then, in mortal fear, spends all her earnings on fortune tellers and amulets.

As if I had been thinking aloud, Marcus Anicius exclaimed, "What kind of world are we living in? What is happening?"

I shrugged. "Peace on earth through reason and order no longer has any appeal to the imagination. That possibility has been rejected."

"The barbarians and the Church are leading Rome down the road to ruin. We turn into barbarians to be free of the demand for reason and responsibility, and at the same time we become Christians so that we can believe in eternal salvation."

"Barbarians, Christians... What do those words mean? There are Gauls and Britons here who are more civilized in the Greek sense than we ever were. The Christian sects engage in a life and death struggle over the Holy Trinity and Transsubstantiation; they would rather make a monstrous alliance with the most decadent pagans than reach out to those they call apostates and heretics — are these the followers of the Galilean? The Church which calls itself catholic is more interested in exercising temporal power than in bringing salvation to souls. The so-called barbarians want more than anything else to

live as Romans. And we — you and I — what are we?
Impotent heirs to something that was once great in
its clarity and efficacy but that now has been crushed
under a weight of senseless formalities, a pompous
muddle. Those who are stronger and more ambitious than we will lift this burden from our shoulders."

"But let us act!" He began to pace up and down
beneath the double row of narrow columns around
the rain basin. "For a moment I wasn't sure. . .
you've changed so much physically. But your tongue
doesn't lie; you haven't lost the gift of eloquence.
Listen, in the name of the friendship which my two
nephews felt for you —"

"A friendship which couldn't withstand certain
rumors. They didn't want to be my friends at the
time when I needed them most. Think, Marcus
Anicius, you have such an excellent memory. Elo-
quent or not, I have no voice; nobody speaks to me
any more."

He did not look at me. "I don't know any longer.
I've never attached any importance to rumors. A
man of honor relies on what he sees himself and on
what happens to him."

I gazed at his reflection in the shallow water, while

he spoke.

"At that time, you were isolated, excluded from public life by an indefensible judgment, the Prefect's treachery. Your name became the name of a dead man. And you have resigned yourself to oblivion," he cried, once more with sudden vehemence. "You endure a nameless existence among nameless people. I could not do that. There is only a degree of difference between your fate and mine. I can still come and go as I please, I have my own property at my disposal, I bear my name with honor. But you know, don't you, that I'm no longer a Senator? The title wasn't taken from me, but since the rules were tightened, Senators who do not accept the established Church are not admitted to sessions.

"I see my old friends dying one by one or retiring to the country. I no longer have any contact with the official world outside this house — or what they call the 'world' these days. What shall I do then — take refuge in philosophy? I have always admired writers for their knowledge, for the meaning that their works can give to the reality of our daily life, to our aspirations, our actions. I'm a man of action — isolation, contemplation, are not in my nature. If I had your gift, your powers of persuasion, I could find

words that would compel my contemporaries —
those who share my beliefs — to listen. Won't you
lend me your voice?"

His tone was supplicating; he came close to me
again.

I put my finger to my lips and shook my head,
signalling that as far as his plea went, I was mute.

"Perhaps it's just as well that your statue was
destroyed," he said bitterly. "You're throwing away
the chance to restore your reputation. Yes, because
you are the creature who in the eyes of Rome glorified the exploits and posturings of the man whom
we have to thank for our misery — Stilicho, who first
played the priests' game and then tried to sell the
Empire to the barbarians —"

"*Et tu, Brute?*" I cried, suddenly remembering that
Marcus Anicius Rufus had been one of those Senators who, in extraordinary session, had decided to
murder Stilicho. "What you say is a lie and you
know it! If ever anyone remembers the reign of
this Honorius, who returned today with so much
fanfare and incense, it will be because of the years
that he relied on Stilicho —"

"You still defend him? You put your muse at his
service, you immortalized his campaigns, defended

his politics, praised him and his wife to the skies. And yet he betrayed you — his treachery toward you was a thousand times worse than anything my nephews Olybrius and Probinus did, and all those who abandoned you — all put together!"

I wrapped myself in my cloak, pulling part of it over my head. I was ready to go out into the night. It was rude of me to cut off his argument like that, but I could not speak about Stilicho. For a long time it was quiet. Then I heard the silver ball jingle in the bowl.

"As you wish," he said. "One thing is good — this will not last much longer. A few years more and my consciousness will be extinguished. I don't want to go on witnessing this degradation. Sometimes I think about Socrates — when he was dying, he charged his friends to offer a cock to Aesculapius in thanks for the healing, the deliverance, which death would bring to him."

At that moment the door to the *tablinum* slid open; the slave who had ushered me in asked his master what he wanted. I did not hear Marcus Anicius's reply, and when the man left I started to follow him. Marcus Anicius stopped me. "One moment."

I turned aside and waited. We did not exchange another word. The slave reappeared and handed me a scroll in a cylinder.

4.

I, who have sworn never again to put pen to paper except to teach the illiterate to read and write, behave as if nothing has happened. No, that's not true. It's impossible to imagine a greater contrast between the past and the present. The Imperial clerk, busily composing his work in the palace libraries, a sort of high functionary, official magistrate of the poetic art, no longer exists. I am surrounded by the four walls of my tenement hole. Through the door, which I have to leave ajar in order to get a little light, seeps the stink of pickled fish and of the cesspool beneath the stairs. The gods of Olympus would not feel at home here.

But what is left to write about, now that the lofty scribbling in the service of the Empire is a thing of the past? I am surprised and disturbed by this sudden need to put into words what has happened to me over the last few days. The silence — the refusal to go beyond the here and now — which has become second nature to me, is broken. I realize that for ten long years I have considered myself to be worthless

— if by "myself" one means the series of metamorphoses that I have undergone since my youth, from the barefoot Egyptian country boy to the famous writer of flattery whose verses were as stiff with glittering metaphors as his tunics were with embroidery, and, finally, the pedagogue, under his various surnames, who teaches the seedy residents of his quarter to read and write.

Everything is immediate and inevitable, as well as richer in possibilities, viewed from street level; he who stands on a pedestal does not see what is happening at his feet. The sausage makers, tanners and blacksmiths in the Subura react no differently from the occupants of the palaces of the *clarissimi* and *illustrissimi* — except that the former do not have the slightest interest in hiding or disguising their feelings; they curse, kick, kiss, weep, scold, with complete abandon. They lack self-control because they have not learned to think about it. But at least with them one does not find the hypocritical exploitation of self-control which often follows awareness of it. Their hatred, as well as their affection, is expressed openly, with noisy violence; but it is less dangerous than intrigue.

As I write these words, one of the innumerable

daily disputes is exploding on a lower floor; the stairwell is filled with the screeching of women and children and the sound of dishes breaking. At moments like these I do perhaps look back wistfully at the cool galleries and cypress-lined avenues where once, in tranquility, far removed from filth and discomfort, I could ponder appropriate metaphors for a panegyric. But *this* is reality, *this* has given meaning to my life. My place is here in the ant hill of the Subura—thanks, perhaps, to what I carry within me without conscious memory: the life experiences of my parents and grandparents — slaves, tillers of the soil of the Delta or the Fayyum, accustomed to windowless mud huts and the stench of the dunghill.

My twilit room is stifling; my few possessions (a little cheap paper, writing gear for teaching, a lamp, a winter tunic hanging from a nail in the wall) are also the only moveable objects in the room: the stone bench serves as bed, chair and table. It has been ten years since I last held in my hand anything as luxurious as the *volumen* in which I am now writing. I can't eradicate the seal, in the upper left-hand corner, stamped with the initials of Marcus Anicius Rufus.

I should perhaps have turned tail, should have bolted from the procession when his cortege was moving through the Forum of Trajan. I knew that the confrontation with him would be an ordeal in many respects. I thought above all of the possibility of being recognized, of an unexpected reaction on my part. At the same time, I *wanted* to be recognized. But whatever I had expected, it was surely not this: a scroll of blank parchment between two ivory cylinders — a gift that was a challenge, a goad. And my response to it was the feverish urge to consign to that parchment the experiences, minute by minute, of a single day — the day of the second entry of Honorius.

There was a singular element of repetition in these events, as if I had lived through them once before. I know why: what happened to me was part of a network of various possibilities which, in the days of fame and tranquility, I had rather playfully envisaged. I had asked myself, when I was proceeding to the Forum at the Emperor's side during his first entry, how that magnificent spectacle should strike me if I were watching it as a disillusioned outsider. And when the Roman magistrates unveiled my statue in the midst of the immortals, I saw in my mind's eye that marble in ruins, that place empty.

5.

Stilicho and Serena — they seemed to me to be demigods, the most powerful people in the realm of the Emperor Theodosius. When, on the recommendation of Mallius Theodorus, I was appointed to Stilicho's personal staff, I obtained a privileged post. I lived in Milan, in his house which was part of the Imperial palace. The old Emperor doted on his family: always, wherever he was, he was surrounded by relatives. He looked upon his niece Serena as his own daughter and therefore on her husband as his son.

It was claimed later that Stilicho had cleverly exploited a private conversation with the dying Emperor to have himself named guardian to Theodosius's two sons — seventeen-year-old Arcadius and ten-year-old Honorius. There were no witnesses; no one could disprove it. Rufinus claimed the guardianship of Arcadius and dominion over the Eastern Empire, but everyone knew that Rufinus was a scoundrel. Even if it were true that Stilicho had contrived his appointment, he was still in the

right: he acted in the spirit of the Emperor who had
lived long enough in Constantinople to be well
acquainted with the courtiers and eunuchs — their
appetite for luxury, their corruption, their mutual
spitefulness — and who wanted above everything to
maintain the unity of the Empire.

Although he was widely respected and admired,
Stilicho was not loved. Many of those who praised
him the loudest — because they needed him — must
actually have hated him. He gave an impression of
infallibility; he never seemed to make a mistake and
he appeared in complete control of every situation —
people will not forgive such perfection. He was in
perfect health, indefatigable; in middle age, he still
looked like a young man. And, in addition, he had
a disarmingly naive air that had often struck me
among people of his race. He had the easy manner
of a man of the world; he had, after all, grown up in
a villa on the Bosphorus, near the Eastern capital
where his father was a military functionary at the
Imperial court.

His hair and eyes were light, but he had the
smooth brown skin of a Greek, not the Vandal's
ruddy complexion. He spoke Greek and Latin
without an accent; I believe he could not understand

his father's language. I used that in a poem as an argument defending him against the repeated accusation that he maintained secret contact with the chiefs of the Vandal hordes on the Thracian frontier.

He never allowed himself to appear ridiculous; he had an undeniable air of authority. There were many who resented that: one of the deepest grievances against him was undoubtedly the fact that it was impossible to look down on him, even though he was of foreign origin and *homo novus*. His worst enemy could not accuse him of stupidity.

In Stilicho I saw the embodiment of what, since my childhood, I considered true masculinity, qualities which I myself aspired to: calm courage, self-assurance without bravado, a dislike of deceit and corruption which was genuine and not rooted, as with so many people, in hypocrisy. What has been called his "twisting and turning", his unpredictability, came, I believe, from the nature of his intelligence. He saw everything in a wider context than most people; his idea of reality encompassed much more than the narrow reality of others.

When I first came to Rome, I thought that currents of opinion and political factions should be easily recognizable. I did not have the slightest idea of the diversity and complexity of the possibilities for and against the Emperor's policies, for or against the Church, for or against what you will. Those who are friends and companions today become sworn enemies tomorrow and vice versa. Personal feuds transcend group interests. Words and deeds are seldom in accord with each other.

Stilicho had continually to deal with all those personalities and all those opinions; to become explicitly involved in those relationships and internal situations was self-defeating; the only result could be deadlock. One made oneself vulnerable when one supported one man or one party. But as important as all these things seemed (because one was close to them), they hardly counted for Stilicho in comparison with real problems: how to prevent the threatened rupture between the Occidental and the Eastern Empires, how to stop the aggressive barbaric tribes on the northern frontier from taking advantage of unrest at home. He was able on short notice to bring opposing factions together so he could resolve difficulties as quickly as possible. There were few who understood this, and later, after his death, there were fewer still who appreciated what he had accomplished in spite of everything.

Time after time he was frustrated by treachery, lack of understanding, born stupidity or the blind hatred felt toward him by members of the Senate and the court. Without lightning-quick responses and an ability to take the long view, he would not have been able to succeed as often as he did. And it was those who were closest to him (Theodosius, Honorius, Serena and, in a certain sense — alas! — I myself, his personal poet) who were the first to oppose him.

I have never been at a loss for words, but a feeling of impotence verging on despair seizes me whenever I attempt to express the complexity and ambiguity of my attitude toward Stilicho. I wish that I could be dignified and pragmatic as a true Roman and declare my deep-seated allegiance to everything clear, correct and well-ordered . . . and I wish that the intellect and the ability to integrate and deduce that I owe to my Greek education had granted me the calm certainty that, under the sun that lights the world of mortals, everything can be explained. But I am neither Roman nor Greek.

Although Serena was small and slender, she was imposing because of her bearing and her choice of dress and ornaments. It is impossible to imagine greater elegance. She aspired to perfection in everything that she undertook. She had a passion for beautiful and costly things (a characteristic that had brought Stilicho more than once to the verge of bankruptcy). In addition she possessed naturally what Proba, the mother of the Anicii (often considered her rival) had never succeeded in acquiring, despite her zealous efforts: a strong aptitude for learning and fine taste in the arts.

He who has never seen Serena reading or playing the zither, leaning back in her chair amidst flowering oleanders, the asymmetrical folds of her gown — in crocus yellow and violet — flowing from shoulder to hip, from knee to foot; with cameos at her throat and in her hair — he who has never seen Serena thus will never be able to appreciate the inordinate grace of a Roman noblewoman. However one could not call her amiable in the usual sense of that word. She was royally generous to her favorites, royally harsh toward those who no longer pleased her, royally capricious and royally self-willed about those whims, as if she were the only person in the world.

Some of her friends, after they had become Christians, decided to convert their property to cash and give it to the poor. Without hesitation, Serena offered a fortune for their palaces, parks and art treasures. But at that moment Stilicho did not have the requisite amount of money; he was forced to break the bargain. It was he who was blamed, while Serena was forgiven in advance.

Then there was the affair of the *Magna Mater*. Did *I* plant that outrageous notion in Serena's head? Once, half in jest, half from a desire to flatter her, I said she was the only woman on earth worthy of wearing the priceless necklace which, on ceremonial days, decorated the neck of the goddess.

At that time there were many who, influenced by the bishops, openly voiced their suspicions of Stilicho — he was suspected of being in league with Eugenius, the candidate for emperor of the non-Christian party — and conspired to destroy him. After Eugenius was defeated in a brief campaign (Theodosius's last), Stilicho had to prove his loyalty to the Christian party. Serena, who from childhood had stayed on friendly terms with the families of non-Christian Senators, received her customary invitation to attend the annual festival of the *Magna Mater* as honored guest.

She went there and sat in the front row, wearing a rich garment; it was noted that she wore no jewels. At the highest point of the ceremonies, she stood up, took the five-strand golden necklace from the statue of the goddess and hung it around her own neck. Those who were present said later that all the women were paralyzed with terror and remained frozen in their places. Serena walked out of the temple, followed by her companions.

I saw her coming from where I was waiting with the rest of the retinue of Stilicho's household. She was white as chalk; her eyes were glassy; she was propping up the necklace with both hands to ease the weight of those rows of heavy golden beads. What could one read in her face? Pride, defiance, understandable excitement, perhaps even the awareness that she was more beautiful than ever with this ornament which no mortal woman before her had ever worn. But she looked like a corpse, like her own ghost. Her face resembled the face that I recognized in horror many years later, in the bloody debris nailed to the Aurelian wall.

At the time I heard some worshippers of the gods say that in perpetrating that shameless theft, she had drawn the executioner's axe to her own neck. What is certain is that from that day forward many very influential Senators nourished a deadly hatred toward her; others, who were not attracted to any

particular form of religion and who understood her
secret motivation nevertheless openly deplored her
lack of tact. All the blame was flung at Stilicho,
although it was said that he had not known what
she was going to do. But the result of that bizarre
act was the opposite from what she had intended:
the Christians mistrusted Stilicho more than ever.

Nearly some ten years later, with her sharp femi-
nine intuition, she had a presentiment which no
one — I least of all — had even dreamt of: that my
luck had changed; that I had become a millstone
around Stilicho's neck.

I was known far and wide as Stilicho's poet.
Anything that put *me* in an unfavorable light had to
hit him twice as hard. His attempt to come to an
accord with the neighboring Goths (he knew that
Rome stood no chance in a war) had shocked both
Honorius's Christian and non-Christian advisors
into frantic opposition. Serena understood that at
that moment Stilicho could ill afford a scandal
centering around his eulogist. With the resourceful-
ness and energy that was characteristic of her, she
succeeded in recruiting a bride for me in Libya (a
respectable distance from Rome) along with a position there: the first was a guarantee that I would not

abandon the second.

She caught me off-balance with these accomplished facts. Her attitude was affable but relentless.
Stilicho was with the court in Ravenna; I have never
known whether he was aware of this plan of Serena's. In a final attempt to soften her, I dedicated a
poem to her in which I thanked her for all the favors
she had shown me and pleaded for the opportunity
to return to the city. Something must have leaked out
about my imminent departure: not long after that,
I was arrested. While I write, I am struck by the
form of this essay: I am writing it as if it were a letter
(as I presently write so many letters in the names of
others — relating experiences, arguing, explaining)
to a reader whom I do not know. Is this perhaps
myself? What do I have in common with the man
who vanished ten years ago in the dungeons of the
prefecture? Who was Claudius Claudianus?

Claudius Claudianus: who, what? An exceptional
mastery of the poetic art. A mind steeped in the
exercises of the *Progymnasmata* of Libanius. An
imagination which accepts confinement to stated
themes and prescribed forms. A luxuriant vocabu-
lary, a striking ability to improvise. An ideal product

of the schools of rhetoric in Alexandria.

Claudius Claudianus: ten whole years — no more — reckoned from the moment I set foot on the shore at Ostia to the moment at which I was condemned to vanish from society. An existence by the grace of those whose praises I sang. I myself not to be found in any of these verses, unless in the personages of Stilicho, Serena, Honorius, Rufinus, Eutropius, Gildo, heroes and villains into whom I blew the breath of life; or behind the allegorical figures, the gods and goddesses, the whole mythological puppet show which I gathered around my human subjects in order to elevate them above a drab, unheroic reality.

Claudius Claudianus: A moment of awakening, once, on the Alpine slopes, at the first dazzling sight of ice. A frozen mountain stream, crystal fringes hanging from the rocks, chains of cold lace — this made me aware of what poetry really is: living emotion, rendered in a form allied to ice; flowing, elusive, imprisoned in something hard but transparent, colorless but reflecting all the colors in the rainbow. Before this shimmering display, I stood as if I were nailed to the earth. From that moment, I no longer believed in what I did whenever I put pen to paper.

Claudius Claudianus: he who, despite all this, continued to write verses. Betrayal of the ice crystal of poetry. At the same time betrayal of something else: of the bright inner lucidity from which poetry springs. From the ice cold clear light, I turned back to Milan-on-the-plain. I forgot what I had discovered — worse still, I repudiated it.

Claudius Claudianus: the ambitious, zealous architect of a composition in black and white about the power struggle between the western and the eastern parts of the Empire, Stilicho against Rufinus. I put my imagination at the service of politics. In order to justify Stilicho's angry aversion to the *praefectus praetorio Orientis*, I inflated Rufinus's hatred for Stilicho to the dimensions of a natural catastrophe. I convinced myself as I wrote. Once convinced, I set out to win over others. The verses, recited in the Senate and the court, copied and disseminated, had a great success. On the authority of Claudius Claudianus, Rufinus was referred to far and wide as a monster.

Claudius Claudianus: when, far away in Constantinople, Rufinus was murdered by a handful of soldiers, torn apart and the pieces carried through the streets for the edification and amusement of the populace — the head here, a hand there — I used this nasty story in order to praise Stilicho once more. The result was a storm of rumors: Stilicho had had his most dangerous rival in the Empire put out of the way.

Precisely because I did not believe for a moment that Stilicho was really involved in the murder, and because I was convinced (by whispers among some insiders) that other enemies of Rufinus had cleverly exploited the prevailing mood, I decided to make a virtue of necessity and give Stilicho the full responsibility for the assassination. I considered it an audacious move. In order to present that act as acceptable, necessary — even righteous — I needed only to paint in the blackest colors the abyss of depravity which had engulfed the late Rufinus and others — still living, no less dangerous rulers — in the Eastern Empire and elsewhere.

Claudius Claudianus: he who had taken a step on the road from which there was no turning back. When gods fall from their pedestals, those who have created those gods cannot watch with impunity. The day would have to come when I would realize that Stilicho was a man like other men, not the

Apollonian upholder of justice and order which I had made him seem, the hero without fear or blemish; that he could make mistakes, sometimes had unclean hands and often remained silent when frankness would complicate the situation.

There did indeed come a time when I could no longer swallow this behavior of his because it cast a shadow on the image which I had shaped in my poems and in which I actually believed. In the epic climate of my verses he might be the avenger who had saved the world from Rufinus: but in reality I could not bear the idea that he had most probably given the order for the murder when he learned that others were plotting to do it. There was no certainty of this, all suppositions were possible, but especially those unfavorable to him. However, he still elicited admiration; he could not be accused of deceit, even under the surface. Everything was different from what one believed. This put my occupation in a different light. *He* appeared to shake off these dark questions with ease; they clung to *me*.

I could not in fact forgive him for that, any more than I could forgive Serena for the coldness at her core, her calculating nature — this was the creature whom I had once glorified in an ode: "O *maxima*

rerum gloria! O glory of the world!" I doubted
Stilicho and Serena, but I went on putting my work
at their service. I did not succeed in detaching
myself from them with the ease with which they
later rid themselves of me. My statue had already
been erected in the Forum of Trajan.

Claudius Claudianus: This marble doll, a symbol
of the poetic spirit, bore only a surface resemblance
to the crystal of poetry; in substance it was colder
and harder than the Alpine ice.

The condemned man who was taken under military guard beyond the hundred-mile marker outside
Rome, was no longer Claudius Claudianus — nor
was the tramp who, under cover of the chaos created
by the Gothic occupation, returned to his beloved
City.

And after that? After that I (the unknown, the
nameless, born on the banks of the Nile) began to
learn what life is. No theory, no convention, not the
formality of court life where (as any keen observer
can see) anarchy prevails. Ordinary people: men
who practice their trade in the workplace as long as
it is light, who make good use of years spent in their
youth learning to earn their bread: tanning hides,
woodworking, beating copper, painting, firing pots,

boiling *garum* from fish, weaving cloth. Women who bear children in the caves and cellars where they live, suckle and feed them and do household tasks until the children in their turn stand in the workplace. That is daily reality for the people of Rome.

Since I wanted to make use of the veneer of culture which I had been able to acquire, I opened a school to serve these people. I offered them my ability to set thoughts on paper. I have not been unhappy — on the contrary — but perhaps I should have been because I realized that one man, by himself, cannot alleviate the ignorance — occasionally amusing but nearly always distressing and sometimes even frightful — of thousands of people.

Whenever I emerge from the Subura, I see the villas of rich Christians and I come across a procession led by a priest who is transporting the recently exhumed remains of another holy martyr to one of the basilicas or to a hastily constructed chapel. I can hardly believe my eyes. I ask myself, why this feverish pursuit of the bones of idealists when one could, day after day, hour after hour, make practical application of that idealism by helping to bring about a decent existence for those ragged fellow-creatures huddled in the rat's nest of the Subura? Of course the very poor can be recruited as converts, not by giving them food, but by tricking them into believing that if they pray to the earthly remains shut up in a sarcophagus or shrine (whether these are actually the remains of real martyrs is another question), they can bring about miracles.

I am well acquainted with a handful of Christians here in the quarter who condemn this abuse of credibility (pointing out that it is no different from the most blatant superstitions of the past). These are people whom I respect: they don't make a display of their convictions, but they live their faith. Nothing human is alien to them, and they are unusually cheerful and self-disciplined. I believe that they are much more concerned with examining their own souls than with converting their neighbors. I have no access to their religious life: they do not volunteer any information. It's possible that they are Arians and therefore prudent out of self-protection. But they do not hide: in case of need, they never refuse a call for help.

The Church, with its impressive rituals and clouds of incense, plays no role here in the Subura; no more than the practices of the anchorite, that other emblem of sanctity which is becoming more popular every day. If by chance a monk strays from his cloister or a hermit from his cave, and finds his way to this part of the City, he is jeered at and spat upon because he has fled from the world and has chosen to live in wanton filth.

Life here does not rise above the level of the rooftops; it consists essentially of the pavements, the sewers, the stained and moldy walls, constant din of voices, peddling and squabbling, shrieks of pain and of laughter, stink and smoke, darkness behind the doorways, garbage and stray animals, swarms of adults and children. If this sort of existence changes at all, it changes very slowly. Disruption from outside too, has very little effect here. When the Goths were in Rome, they left the Subura alone. Here I am no longer in the present; I am outside time but up to my neck in material reality. I know so well the power of need; the all-consuming search for basic necessities.

For the first time in many months, I left the labyrinth, impelled by curiosity. Honorius went by, a voice cried "*Munera, Munera!*" between the temples, and suddenly everything changed.

6.

Of course I was followed on the way back from Marcus Anicius's house. Again and again something rustled behind me in the darkness and shot away at an angle whenever I looked back. At first I took it to be a stray dog, but it may well have been the dwarf. When I was leaving the bathhouse yesterday at noon, the fat wrestler popped up out of the crowd at me: I must go with him whether willingly or unwillingly; Pylades wanted to speak with me. I thanked him for the honor and escaped into the bustle of the streets.

Then today the actor himself appeared at the shed next to the fruit market where I was teaching. I let him wait in the hope that he would soon tire of it, but an hour later he was still there, sauntering among the watermelons. In order to get rid of him, I offered him a drink. In the tavern he came out with a proposal: he was looking for an educated man capable of delivering introductory remarks and reciting poetry during his, Pylades', solo performances as the blind Oedipus, Hercules in the burning shirt, the enraged Ajax, Achilles mourning the death of Patroclus.

"I can dance and sing, but I am no intellectual," he said, with false modesty (his eyes remained calculating). "What I need is a man of education and refinement, with the appearance of a philosopher. I'm certain that I've found him."

I reminded him that nowadays only jugglers performed in the theatres; I thought that he was making fun of me. But no.

"In private houses, of course. The authorities allow it. There's a great demand for it. We must manage somehow with whatever is possible: the pay is good."

"I do useful work in a literary area that brings me enough to live on."

"A select public, of literary connoisseurs, or just newly-rich ignoramuses, who are ready to pay for a grain of culture. But always grateful listeners, often in the long run valuable connections, more than ever *now* — if you see what I mean. In the works of the great poets, the gods still live."

"It doesn't appeal to me."

"You're accustomed to quite a different life from this."

"I'm satisfied."

"*I'm* not," he said, with sudden ferocity. He moved nearer to me and lowered his voice. From close by, I saw his wrinkled skin, the black smudges under his eyes. The odor of his pomade was so overpowering that I had to turn away from him.

"I now have a company — what I call a company. The dwarf, the fat man, a girl I picked up in the street. You've seen me perform in the past ..." He put his hand on my sleeve; there were tears in his eyes — a genuine reaction, for the first time. "Can you imagine what it means to me to have to work — when work of that kind is possible today — with a bunch of freaks that don't know the first thing about any of it? I am a professional person and what I am doing now has nothing to do with my profession. I am betraying the artist I once was. It's betrayal enough in my field to grow old, to become decrepit. I am a perfectionist; there is nothing I find so humiliating as being forced to give third-rate performances simply because my troupe doesn't measure up. I spend hours working to prepare myself, I tune my instruments, swallow honey to make my vocal cords supple, do my exercises, paint a mask on my face. It is my practice to leave nothing to chance. But that monster, and the whore, and the fellow who's only good for strong-arming people — they have no conception of finesse. This is eating me up."

"I wouldn't be any better at it than they are, believe me."

"The great classic works, without vulgar sensationalism; the solo mime in the style of the golden age — that's what I want to bring back. I'll drop the troupe. If you lecture on the text, explaining and making connections —"

"That's absolutely out of the question."

"I can force you to do it," he said, with sudden venom.

"I don't believe that."

"Don't be so sure of yourself. It could be in your own best interests to do what I ask of you. There are greater stakes involved here than just mine, that's all I can tell you right now."

I thought that this was enough, and I left him. He called something after me but I could not make it out.

A couple of days passed. Yesterday, when I came home toward evening, I could hear the rustle of the straw mattress behind the door to my room. I pushed the door open but at first in the half-light I could make out nothing. Then I saw someone sitting on my bed. As I snatched up the lamp and struck it into flame, I demanded that the visitor identify himself. Breathing and rustling, but no response. The wick flamed up.

A woman was huddled in the farthest corner of my couch. I saw, between the reddish strands of hair, the pale gleam of her arms and shoulders, and lower, her *palla*, which had slipped into a muddle of saffron-colored folds. I asked her what she wanted, why she hadn't replied. She made no sound, but glowered at me from behind her hair. I took her arm to pull her out of the corner; her clothing glided still farther down her body. She kept staring at me, with a mixture of defiance and distrust. She gathered her garments about her — or appeared to, for I had the impression that she was baring herself with every movement. I recognized her now; she was the woman I had seen in the public house on the day of Honorius's entry, the mistress or accomplice of Pylades and his cohorts. I was angry because I saw through this new scheme: since neither promises nor threats had worked with me, they had sent me a woman, thinking that I, poverty-stricken and long in the tooth, would be so eager for her free favors that I would not be able to resist yielding to them.

"Get out of here or I'll throw you out!"

I expected her to curse or spit as she had the first time. But she said nothing, drew up her shoulders, and then looked suddenly helpless and forlorn as she groped for her sandals on the floor in front of the couch. I felt the same pity for her that I feel for the grimy children on the staircase of the *insula*, who creep up to me to show me their scratches after a scuffle or a beating, or to beg a crust of stale bread.

"What's your name?" I asked, pushing one of her sandals toward her with my foot.

"Urbanilla," she said, sullenly.

"Urbanilla, I don't want you. Tell that to Pylades. He must leave me in peace."

She stooped to fasten her shoes, looking at me over her shoulder. Eyes like stone. The flame of the oil lamp trembled in a draught, shadows moved like dark water over her back and thighs, over the curve of her arm, coming to rest on the edge of the couch.

It was as if I saw, against the backdrop of the

plaster wall, a sphinx or harpy from the house of Olympiodorus in Alexandria; one of the life-sized female monsters now become flesh and blood: an ageless face, a blind stare, half-open mouth filled with darkness, a torso with youthful breasts, the lower body fallen into folds and coils which evoked the indistinct forms of plants, billows, animal claws.

These rapid metamorphoses overwhelmed me: first a vulgar streetwalker, then a helpless child and finally something inhuman in human form, a ghastly visitation in the night. I had felt successive aversion, rage, and compassion looking at this creature on my sleeping bench; but all these emotions left me — what remained I cannot describe.

The girl herself was not aware of these metamorphoses—I knew that, of course. She was like clay, or wax being shaped without her own participation, in a form she could not understand. I saw in her everything that could lead a man to ruin: not seduction in the erotic sense, for what was there before me did not promise the satisfaction of lust. It was something else, more than that: the temptation of the unknown, the pursuit of self-created danger, the irrepressible desire to

penetrate into regions where the borders were blur-
red between cruelty and pleasure, life and death,
man and beast.

If I had taken that woman at that moment, I would
perhaps have been able to drive away the images
which swarmed around me, incoherent as dreams
or drunken visions, offering the unheard-of, the
never-seen. . . Unequalled power over the powerless, the possibility of frightful suffering consum-
ing the entire world and all the creatures in it. I
can't put it into words. I don't know why, I
shuddered as if I saw before me a field gnawed
bare by locusts, a mutilated, depopulated city; or,
again, a mob of escaped slaves (I saw them four
years ago when the Goths took Rome) seeking out
their former masters to wreak vengeance on them
for ill-treatment and humiliation. I remembered
the face of Persephone, abducted by the dark god:
beauty touched by death in the full bloom of life.
I saw the Medusa head of the murdered Serena,
stuck on a spear above a Rome fallen into decay.

Now in daylight, it seems to me absurd — clearly
insane — that because she scowled at me, because she
bent over to fasten her sandals, a creature like
Urbanilla could be raised to dizzying heights as

the embodiment of a choice for or against humanity. This lasted, it is true, for only an instant. As soon as she stood erect, she became a young slut like hundreds of others who stroll about in the Subura, indifferently flaunting her naked breasts while slowly lifting her skirts. "What do you want from me?" I asked harshly, in confusion.

"Ask the boss," said the girl, shrugging, before she disappeared.

Recollection of things long forgotten. Once in the reed-lands, I had cut off the head of a cock. A cruel game, a senseless, horrible act. The thrashing and fluttering of the vigorous animal in my grasp, his hoarse shrieks and later the jerking of that headless body, gave me a thrill of curiosity, dislodging something in me — I don't know what — the desire to prove my power, to test the limits of endurance, to fill a black void with violence? Much later, at the house of Olympiodorus, I had had the same feeling; only there *I* was the cock, the object of oppression, who struggled in desperate panic. The only witnesses, the stone harpies. I realize now that this time of darkness affected, in the ensuing years, my closest friendships, thwarting them, undermining them. Concerning men, I knew no middle way between hatred and hero-worship; one woman, Serena — who belonged to Stilicho — I elevated to the role of celestial mother: the others I mounted in cold, heartless lust as if they were the sphinxes on whom I must avenge myself.

The Works of Claudius: lifeless ornamental plants, artificial vines in the darkness.

This afternoon, in the crush of the fruit market, someone nudged me and whispered, "Marcus Anicius Rufus asks that you come, about the fifth hour after sunset; it is very urgent!"

I could not overtake the man.

III.

THE PREFECT

1.

Profound silence in the chamber where the Prefect has retired for his afternoon rest. Sun shades temper the light. Outside, in the cypress trees of the neglected garden of the temple of Tellus, the crickets have begun their shrill monotonous song. The Prefect is stretched out on his couch, but he is not asleep. The unrolled manuscript, draped across his knees, hangs down to the floor. He should feel heavy and languid, as one does after a protracted undertaking has been brought to a successful conclusion. But he is restless and uncomfortably hot, even without his toga. He moves from the cushions to the marble bench where a slight cool breeze wafts from the shade of the cypress trees. He reaches for his writing gear.

Providence (his hand is unsteady) *has bestowed on me, after ten years, the means of executing, in the spirit of the law, a sentence which was at one time incompletely carried out. In the case of* C.C. (he hesitates before inscribing the initials in the wax), *still a pagan in heart and soul. His remarks about the martyrs, the Church, the faithful! Repeatedly insulting the exalted Honorius. His manuscript one long testament of scorn, tedium vitae, defeatism. Left to himself he has fallen back among the scum of society. The manuscript contains more than enough evidence of the inclinations of Marcus Anicius Rufus, which constitute a danger to the security of the state. This releases us from the necessity of delving into the question of last night's gathering.*

Concerning Pylades and associates: very imprudent, not to say reckless. That soulless trash is really useless. Make short shrift of them. The woman U. held for now in secure custody. Rigorous interrogation? No word about me. Digressions about everything and everyone, allusions to the cesspool in Alexandria, but no word about who rescued him from there, saved his soul from eternal damnation, enabled him to achieve the status he sought so that he could associate with the marvellous, treacherous top dogs. Not a word.

With a spatula, the Prefect smooths over the wax of the writing tablet, wiping out the words he has just written. He presses his fists against his closed eyes (elbows on the table) — a prematurely aged man, but with something immature in the shape of his neck and shoulders and his slender hairless arms. His secretary, who comes to fetch him about the fourth hour of the afternoon, finds him in that position.

"*Clarissime*, it's time. Your toga. . ."

2.

The Prefect of the City to Marcus Anicius Rufus, Marcellinus Maximus, Flaccus Vescularius, Gaius Agirius Flestus, Quintus Fulcinius Trio:

"From everything that I learned during the interrogation this morning, from the Commandant of the City guard, Aulus Fronto, and from the witnesses as well as from you yourselves, combined with evidence contained in a manuscript that has just come to light (written on paper from the library of Marcus Anicius Rufus) by the so-called Niliacus, formerly known as Claudius Claudianus, who for ten years remained illegally in Rome — I believe that it is clear without further discussion that there has been a violation of the law promulgated by the late Emperor Theodosius in the seventeenth year of his reign, Codex Sixteen, Title Ten, Article Two: 'The erection of altars with the intention of bringing sacrifices thereto is forbidden as an attack upon the true religion.' Your culpability is established, in addition, by the sense of paragraph three of the same law: 'Anyone who tolerates such preparations in his own house or in that of another is as guilty as if he had in fact made sacrifices.' Finally, I cite redundantly one of our State's fundamental laws: 'Those who by the inspection of entrails or other idolatrous practices, attempt to discover the future of Sovereign and State have made themselves guilty of a capital offense.'

"Only a few years ago, it would have been my duty to sentence you to death. Thanks to the ordinances issued by the exalted Emperors Honorius and Arcadius in the seventh year of their reign, I can now, for violating the prohibition against holding a gathering after the ninth hour of the afternoon, impose on each of you the penalty of paying thirty pounds in gold. And for your intention to offer sacrifices and consult oracles, I punish you with banishment from Rome for the rest of your lives and the confiscation of all of your possessions in the City and in a radius around it of one hundred miles. There is no appeal against this judgment. It will be carried out immediately."

The condemned men have been ushered out; most of the Prefect's officials leave the building.

Claudius Claudianus has been shut up in a

dungeon, alone, to await his final trial. The Prefect has a discussion with those who are in charge of arranging for the expulsion of the five patricians and the confiscation of their property.

3.

Later the Prefect descends the staircase to the vaults. This reality is stranger than a dream. He had not wanted this second confrontation with him whom that morning he had not recognized – had not wanted to recognize – to take place in the hall with the black-and-white floor, nor in the room set aside for private audiences. Preceded by guardsmen with torches, he penetrates to the lower regions. What he is doing is both useless and unorthodox – he knows that. Wrapped in his white toga, he stands outside the iron bars, staring at the vague figure in the corner, and with a nod signals the guardsmen to move into the background.

"Claudius."

No reply.

"As always, I feel responsible for you."

The man in the cell moves a few steps closer, but not close enough for the Prefect to distinguish his features. "The responsibility of the magistrate in this case applies only to the execution of the delayed sentence," he says.

"The Christian prevails over the magistrate. I

want to save you."

"I haven't asked for mercy."

"It's not a question of what you've asked for; it's a question of the salvation of your soul."

"Is this intended to be reparations for a judicial error? Am I going to be set free?"

"There's no question of error. I will give you your life. Not your freedom."

"Then I prefer that you slice my head off right now."

"In your case you would not be entitled to death by the sword. A pagan, born a slave outside Rome, suspected of criminal activities, soothsaying. . . Such a person usually receives the pyre."

"Into the fire then, like the Phoenix."

"Your recklessness would be ridiculous if it were not so tragic."

"The mime Pylades seemed willing to involve me in the performance of tragedies in more than one sense, in the service of this so-called justice. It would have been a real tragedy if I had let myself be recruited."

"Your insinuations are as empty as an actor's bombast. That actor, by the way, will never boast again — steps have been taken to see to that."

"Undoubtedly similar steps were in fashion ten years ago when I was arrested in Mallius Theodorus's house."

"Don't forget that you were surprised in the act of burying the remains of a sacrificial cock. Those circumstances constituted overwhelming evidence."

"There were indeed sacrifices."

"Of course you helped Mallius to escape in time."

"Sometimes one does something for one's friends. One comes to their rescue even if one has reason to suspect that an informer has had a hand in the summons — as happened last night."

The Prefect paces back and forth before the bars. The prisoner is now standing flush against the barrier; the glimmer of the torches — held aloft at a distance by the guardsmen — illuminates his face, a grimy bearded mask. A criminal in cheap, filthy clothing. The Prefect could not recognize the spirit which had enlivened that other face, of earlier days, which he had been thinking about since that morning.

"Sometimes one does something for one's friends, you say. Who knows that better than I? Haven't I given you enough proof? I can still do something for you. In those days you refused to listen to reason; you would not be converted. Perhaps now I can help to awaken the better man in you, to save your soul. I haven't given up hope. That manuscript of yours which was brought to me — it breathes bitterness. Rome isn't lost! Listen, only the true religion has the power to deliver us, to waken the dead, to breathe new life into what seems to have become old and finished. Only the true faith can inspire City and Empire, can bring peace, order, justice and glory! All resistance will be crushed, reduced to ashes in the fire of our zeal. The new Rome is rising now from idolatrous Rome, for those who have eyes to see and ears to hear —"

"God's State on earth, but the spirit has been driven from it. What is left is the deified State."

"That sounds like heresy. In your manuscript you mention acquaintances of yours in the Subura whom you take to be Arians. That would certainly interest an ecclesiastical court. I don't consider myself qualified to render judgment in those kinds of cases. I could turn you over to that court. . ."

"The Prefect of the City has my fate in his hands."

"You acknowledge that I am powerful?"

"Very powerful. In spite of the coming of the Goths, or perhaps precisely because of it, your career is rising steadily."

"In contrast to most of your former friends, I resigned my office when the City was occupied."

"That gave you more time to devote to the management of your own affairs."

"Still that sarcastic tone. I have maintained my property, provided for my inferiors, met the responsibilities of my class, while you — you risked your skin by coming back to occupied Rome, didn't you? — according to your own words — you crept into that stinking hotbed of the Subura, where you felt at home —"

"Doesn't the wealthy Hadrian own some tenement houses there — as an investment? There is gold to be earned in all that stench."

"You haven't changed. Once again you want to ridicule me, to place me in an unfavorable light. . . ."

"Seize another man's goods. Drive *curiales* to desperation and then profit from their misery. Buy barbarian prisoners of war cheap and then resell them at a profit to work in the copper mines. Buy parcels of land from bankrupt farmers at ridiculous prices so that you can add them to your own holdings. Use heavy fines and severe regulations in certain districts to exercise a reign of terror among artisans who are barely earning a crust of bread, so that you and people like you can profit more from having the work done by your own slaves. And while you are doing all this, kneel three times a day — if not more — in basilicas and chapels and recruit disciples for a new Rome flooded with the light of grace!"

"In the past you asked me to forgive your sarcasm. You called it a youthful sin. Do you expect leniency again?"

"I expect nothing. When I apologized then, I was appealing to that good relationship that you kept talking about all the time."

"It was not I, but you who destroyed that relationship. Where has he gone, he to whom I gave the name Claudius, and who looked up to me with friendship and respect? For admit it — you were grateful to me because I rescued you from Olympiodorus."

"I worshipped you as a god of light — a Mithras, a Helios — that's true."

"Have I ever been anything but a benefactor to you?"

"A god who wants to be worshipped like the sun should not come too close to his worshippers."

"Who's talking about worshipping? The protection I offered you was disinterested, not like that beast —"

"When Olympiodorus — worse than a beast, believe me, because he knew what he was doing — necromancer, lustful torturer, cheat and much more still — When he saw that I was useless for his private pleasure, he offered me work in his library so that I could accept his hospitality without shame as long as I needed to."

"Do you dare to compare *me* to Olympiodorus? Have you ever felt shame in my house, in my company?"

The guardsmen, holding the torches in this central vault from which the cells emerge, can hear from behind them the voices of the Prefect and the prisoner. As disciplined members of the *vigiles*, they force themselves not to listen. They cannot quit their posts; they have to hold the torches high so that the light will penetrate the cell. They try to think about other things: they are not interested in lawsuits, nor in the personal problems of the prisoners or the officials they deal with. It is only when the Prefect issues an order that they turn automatically and stand to attention.

"Fetch the wench Urbanilla."

The prisoner, who has a view of the passage leading to the adjoining dungeons, sees a vague glimmering light, hears a jingling as of countless little metal plates. It is the Great Goddess in an archaic panelled skirt, breasts and arms hung with gold, eyes outlined to large glittering ovals, staring fixedly like a statue. It looks, too — he draws in his breath — like Serena, when she stumbled out of the temple, guilty and victimized, both hands raised to the stolen jewelry, unaware that she had been ordained to die.

She stops quite close to him, the comedian Urbanilla in her messy costume, pale, wide-eyed, her filthy strands of hair in a sticky tangle. The gilded strings and beads sparkle on her heaving breasts but she shows no sign of fear. She jerks herself free from the guard and rubs her upper arm.

The Prefect barely deigns to look at her. With an expression of distaste, he turns once more to the man behind the bars.

"Let us look at the state of your sense of shame. Let us now examine your refined desires and pleasures." To Urbanilla. "You will be subjected to the most rigorous interrogation if I catch you in a lie. Do you know this man?"

"Yes. The schoolmaster."

"How do you know him?"

"Through the boss — Pylades."

"You've seen him in the Subura. What did he say?"

"About the sun, the moon, the stars. About a fellow on a raft at sea and a giant with one eye. About how the black people of Africa hunt elephants. About — about Seneca — or whatever her name is."

"To you?"

"To those boys."

"Which boys? Where?"

"Under the awning next to the fruit market where they learn."

"I mean, what did he say to you when you went with him in the insula Iulia?"

"Who knows?"

"What did he want from you?"

"Nothing."

"You slept with him."

"No."

"Then surely some playfulness and caresses. . ."

"No."

"That's what you came for, wasn't it?"

"I was sent."

"Don't try to make me believe that you could not seduce him. A wench like you knows all the tricks."

"I didn't want to. Not with him."

The Prefect is becoming upset. He perceives a subtle change in the attitude of the guardsmen. They stand at proper attention, immobile, but — he suspects — very conscious of the half-naked woman and surely secretly laughing, astonished at the nature of the interrogation.

Worst of all for the Prefect is the silent presence of the other in his barred cage — he who was the cause of this bizarre performance in the first place. The Prefect feels like a character in a farce by Plautus, comically out of place in his robe of office between a seedy poet and a woman of pleasure, revealing with every word what he would give anything not to reveal, looking ridiculous or — worse — possibly pathetic, in his passion. He has descended from those imposing halls with their distinguished symmetry; he should never have left them. Now he must descend further, whether he wants to or not.

"Did he ask for love potions from you, forbidden

practices?"

"Oh no."

At this umpteenth, casual denial, the Prefect is beside himself. In a voice made unrecognizable by rage, feeling dizzy with dismay at his irreparable error, he shouts at her, "Don't lie! You got him where you wanted him, just as you did with all the others!"

Urbanilla looks from the Prefect to the man behind the bars and back again. She takes her time, then drops her lashes over her sharp glance. "He's not like that" — with a gesture of her elbow in the direction of the guardsmen — "not like them there."

The Prefect does not want to ask her precisely what she means. He feels lightheaded, assaulted by a sensation which he scarcely dares to recognize. (The justice hall in Alexandria, the figure of the student Klafthi among the elegant youths who surrounded Olympiodorus. . .at the same time, despite his indignation, he felt intoxicated, under a sort of spell . . . .)

Suddenly, toward that stupid creature Urbanilla, he is seized by a feeling of indifference bordering on generosity. She is uninteresting; an earlier interrogation conducted by the commander Aulus

Fronto has revealed that she had understood nothing about the role that Pylades made her play; she
knows nothing, is nothing, no, she is not dangerous. A strange feeling of satisfaction, which he
pushes aside while he recovers his dignity. No one
is close enough to him to notice the twitch at the
corner of his eye, the nervous trembling of his lips.

"Take her away."

"Where to, Excellency?"

"Let her go."

The torches crackle in their tubes. Under the low
ceiling, each movement, each gesture throws flickering shadows.

"Are you then so obstinate a heathen that you
choose death over the opportunity to convert?"

"As one condemned to imprisonment for life, I
would then become a hermit, a walled-up anchorite
. . . And the dungeons of the prefecture could be a
place for pilgrims to visit. After my death, do you
want to distribute my bones among the faithful?
That prospect doesn't attract me."

"You mock. You are filled with distrust and
disdain for what I and countless others hold most
sacred. I recognize that look and that slight smile.

If there were a chessboard here before you now, you would not look at me. You would avert your face and move one of the pieces while I'm talking to you."

"I think you're dreaming out loud. You think you're talking to somebody else."

"I thought about him this morning. Now I understand why."

"Chessboard. Eliezar? I've never seen anyone else play that game. I didn't know that I resembled him. Maybe those who are born slaves end up looking like their masters. A brand of nature. . ."

"Exactly right! He has put his stamp in your blood, in your soul. *You are his grandson.*"

Now something seems to press down upon the Prefect; it is as if there is a heavy burden on his shoulders which sinks into him, into his chest, crushing his heart: a chunk of marble or granite, a piece of a relief. A thin voice calls out in the distance, or is it only his imagination? Two stone fingers, larger than life, stab through him before raising themselves aloft as though taking an oath.

The other stands motionless behind the bars. When he finally speaks, his voice is very soft. "His grandson. So, never a slave?"

"Both; grandson and slave, through the mother."

"Who said that, and when?"

"Eliezar ben Ezekiel himself, on the day that he arranged in his will for your emancipation."

The prisoner moves back, away from the barrier, withdrawing into the depths of the cell where he had been standing when the conversation began. Now it is the Prefect who grips the iron bars, bringing his face close to the opening in order to see the other, to catch a glimpse of him in the darkness.

"It's appropriate — a life that began with a testament should end with a testament. Order them to bring me writing gear."

"You're not going to die, not for a long time yet."

"You haven't been able to control my life — don't think that now you have power over my death."

"You forget where you are and who I am."

"I know now who *I* am."

"Claudius, in the name of God, convert!"

"Not that name any more. Give me paper, a pen."

"You made a will ten years ago. You bequeathed your poetry to Rome."

"Because I have survived since then, I want to rescind that bequest. I want to make a newer testament."

Undeniably it is the same voice, softer now, but still marked by a natural authority. Hadrian, suddenly reminded of those conversations in Alexandria, yields to something stronger than he, to a consciousness older and more profound than his own. Some moments earlier the man standing a few feet from him in the darkness had seemed to him to be an extension of Klafthi, a Claudius certainly changed but always recognizable in essence. Now that is over. The distance between them can no longer be bridged.

The Prefect turns away, motions to one of the guardsmen, orders him to bring light and writing gear to the prisoner.

4.

In a palanquin, under armed escort, the Prefect is brought back to his villa. After a bath and a hasty meal (alone, silent, served by slaves who move like shadows), he paces back and forth for a while in the *peristylium*. The moon rises, reddish, at first deformed, then growing sharper in contour, a disc of light. In the garden, the leaves begin to gleam. How can he state the grounds, in the morning, for the fact that this one time the customary sentence will not be carried out? Transfer the prisoner from the death cells of the *Tullianum* where he awaits execution, pretend to forget him and, after a decent interval, convey him to a suitable place of custody? Give everyone, including the prisoner, the impression that justice will run its course? Justice?

Suddenly the Prefect is overcome by a devastating feeling of exhaustion. His limbs are as heavy as stone; he still feels the constant pressure in his chest. He lies down on a couch which has been pushed to the edge of the gallery, close to a basin in which the reflection of the moon floats among the water plants. Memories of Canopis and the bright nights on the Nile. Something — a leaf, an insect — has fleetingly stirred the surface, which quivers slightly — fragmented silver. Gazing at it, he must have fallen asleep for a moment; when he wakes with a start, the moon is scarcely higher above the rooftop. Clammy, with pounding heart, he sits on the edge of the couch.

He thinks of the dream which had haunted him yesterday. He knows suddenly who it was who called to him from across the sea. In the dream he was himself a prisoner of the basalt wall; the other had abandoned him, sailing away over the horizon. In reality it was the other way round: the fugitive returned, as if by a miracle, and was imprisoned. But I shall not abandon you, says the Prefect aloud; at the sound of his own voice, he looks about him, startled. It is silent in the galleries. He wants to believe that the cry — "Hadrian!" — was a call for help. Although secretly he knows better, he forces his memory to obey that interpretation: the ship was not sailing away; it was approaching. He himself was not there, alone and destitute on the seashore, waiting. This wait is rewarded. I will not abandon you. I will temper justice with mercy. Justice?

What is justice, what is injustice? whispers the Prefect, desperately attempting once again to substitute the illusion for the dreaded vision. His voice is so low that what he says cannot be heard.

As first magistrate of the City, of course he knows the *regulae juris*, the rules of law. He enjoys showing off his knowledge of them: during hearings he adorns his arguments with citations. At this moment, his memory turns against him, suggesting to him what he least needs under the circumstances — the ancient rule concerning questions of justice and injustice, a theoretical sentence to be chiselled in marble: *Better to free the guilty than to risk the condemnation of the innocent.*

A dissident inner voice attempts to justify the innumerable decisions, which he has made in the past, conflicting with the golden rule. Is it injustice to condemn an atheist for a crime he has not committed? Isn't his impiety enough to render him guilty by definition? Who will deny that his mere existence is pernicious, that everything he does is a crime? Is it unjust to bring about the condemnation of such a person by creating the appearance of guilt, with the intention of purifying the State and society for the greater glory of God? Hasn't a magistrate the right to take preventative measures? Haven't the emperors, over the course of the last two centuries, issued edicts and decrees giving the law greater freedom of action on just this point?

The Prefect stands up, dazzled by the double light of the moon – in the sky above the eaves and in the water at his feet. He moves into the depths of the house, lingers irresolute in one of the apartments between the *peristylium* and the forecourt. He deems himself justified this time in altering a judgment. What is more, it is impossible for him to execute that judgment. But he knows that no lawbook contains a formula which can be used to make his determination acceptable, without at the same time weakening all precedents and stopping the administration of justice – or so it would seem.

From within the gallery (furnished with deceptive austerity: the stiff chairs are fashioned from ivory; the unembellished lamps are silver), he stares at the blue glow in the distance beyond the pillars. He is convinced that he has the right; he has no doubts. At moments like these, the sort of life he leads (*must* lead, he thinks) weighs heavily upon him. What has so often filled him with satisfaction – the sight of his valuable possessions, the knowledge

that he is being served with the deepest submissive-
ness and care —now seems only to emphasize his
solitude.

You shall learn to pray, just as I now go to pray, he
says, half-aloud in the silence, to the other, who is far
out of earshot in the vaults of the prefecture. At first
you will curse the darkness and the isolation, but
then, later, you will acknowledge with gratitude that
this is the only way you could gain insight. For you
will come to realize that the world is only a pretense,
a desert from which those turn away who are truly
saved. When you are desperate, when you need
guidance, I shall be there. In my capacity as Prefect
of the City, I am taking a great risk. I hope that you
appreciate the depth of my friendship.

He wants to rescue the other from his obstinacy
and to restore their initial closeness. The prisoner
will certainly have a strong ongoing aversion to his
environment — that will help him to develop a
completely new perspective. In the brown and green
hills of Umbria, an isolated monastery. If the other,
at some later date, after years of repentance, should
renounce his worldly involvement, and if he himself, after fulfilling his administrative tasks, should
decide to choose a life of retirement from the

world, then perhaps for both of them, a shelter in the pious community of monks. Doing penance, finding redemption. A perfect victory.

Another image intrudes: the worn face of Eliezar ben Ezekiel in the shadows — his sorrowful eyes closed, his head nodding almost imperceptibly while he, Hadrian, reads him the poem about the Phoenix. He remembers his feeling of triumph, hardly tempered by pity, on seeing Eliezar dying, defeated, abandoning his habitual reserve, recognizing Hadrian as a person of consequence. Why else would he have confided to a stranger that secret, the source of his worry and his doubts?

For over twenty years, Eliezar has been in his grave. If he were still alive, how would he approach this ragged schoolmaster from the Subura — his counterpart?

Although the night air is mild, the Prefect trembles with cold. He knows quite well why it is that his body feels as heavy as stone. He wants to cry out, a protracted lament — to call back the Hadrian of an earlier day, not yet rigid, not yet burdened with guilt over injustice and perjury. Standing in his quiet marble house, he begins to grasp the real meaning of his dream.

He spends the rest of the night in his *oratorium*, a closed, bare space, windowless, a cell. He kneels, his head bent, muttering incessantly.

The stars have grown pale when he reappears in the gallery. He wakes a slave, summons his secretary, sends them, despite the early hour, with an urgent message to the hall of justice. Leaning back on his couch — in the garden the flowers and leaves are regaining their colors — he savors the victory which he has won over himself.

Claudius. Now you will be forced to see what you have always stubbornly denied until today — that I am your friend and your benefactor, that I have come forward to help you in your hour of need, that at great personal sacrifice, I have given you your liberty. No one has ever behaved more generously to you. Unthinkable that this act of mine should not convince you. Now it is obvious that your resistance rests on a misunderstanding. You believe that I act only out of self-interest, driven by God knows what predilection to tyranny. But I am the master of my emotions. I am setting you free. You will not be pursued. Go in peace. Of the two of us, I have been the stronger, just as I was stronger than Eliezar. Wherever you are, whatever you do, you will not escape me any longer. Your conscience, all that is best in you, will remain tied to me forever.

Exhausted, he has dropped off to sleep in the early morning. Hadrian! Suspended between dreaming and waking, he feels a deep pleasure, like a sick person who knows that he will soon be cured. Hadrian! *Clarissime!* The voice of his secretary at the foot of his couch. Now he will hear that Marcus Anicius Rufus and his friends have been arrested in the night and transported to the prefecture for a speedy trial. A confused dream crosses his consciousness just on the border where images are created by repressed pain and distress. He no longer knows what it was, nor does he want to know. He opens his eyes.

His secretary is indeed standing there. The message has been delivered. The previous afternoon, on the Prefect's order, wax tablets had been provided to the prisoner, now freed; his writings were retrieved from the cell.

The secretary — correct as always, but behaving with a certain wariness which the Prefect has never noticed in him before — places the bound and sealed tablets at the foot of the couch and, with a bow, departs.

5.

Eliezar, Father —

By way of salutation and of posthumous homage, I dedicate to you this testament which is not one, since I have nothing to leave. I call you father: my life comes from you, you have created it. Your son who begat me, still lives in Alexandria, unreachable. He is nothing to me, I am nothing to him. You, who no longer exist, I can reach only in myself, nowhere else. I scarcely knew you. To me you were the old man, the lord of the estates, immensely rich in possessions and in knowledge, the wise, strong master, taken for granted as the backdrop to my life. My future lay in your hands.

Once, when I came across you in the olive garden, you made a gesture as if you were about to place your hand on my head. But you quickly recovered and simply waved your hand at me. I feared you, I respected you, but at every turn, whenever I saw you — in conversations with overseer or steward, slaves or freed servants, women or children — you were always listening with the same attentiveness, always speaking with the same calm composure, even when it was a question of a reprimand or punishment. This caused me to be overwhelmed by a vague feeling, a mixture of despair and malice, a need to provoke, to push you to the point where I could see you lose that patient self-control, to force you to act in a way that would justify the secret undercurrent of hatred inside me. I was not grateful when you did not punish me after that bloody game with the cock, but instead sent me to school in the city. But I forgot my resentment when I became absorbed in my studies. I did not think about you any more. I worshipped the rector Claudianus who imparted knowledge to me and, through that knowledge, a feeling of dignity. When *he* died, I realized that I stood alone.

Perhaps I knew unconsciously what has never been revealed until today. Flesh of your flesh, blood of your blood, and at the same time irrevocably rejected, shut out. Who knows, I may have spent my life striving, in word and deed, to prove my right to exist. I sought for what I had never really had — a father: example and roots. In the under-world, in the realm of black magic, I found a father-in-evil: Olympiodorus. I wanted to possess the demonic power which I believed was his. Later I saw fathers in people whom I considered to be wise, level-headed, of unimpeachable integrity. At every turn, another image of myself as a "son", a new form of dependency, and then, after a time, new forms of resistance: I must break away in order to go on living.

Now I have outgrown all that; I have passed the age at which I needed to be a son. No more the unconditional surrender, the identification. I don't want any longer, out of shame or self-contempt, to destroy what I once revered. To be adult, independent — that means having the courage to submit one's acts — as well as those of others — to a lucid examination, to criticism; to challenge the self-love, the pretensions of infallibility which are hidden in all of us.

It would seem that, three centuries after the short and promising rebellion under the sign of the Fish (against the rigidity of the Law and Authority, the State and the Faith, and despite internal rigidity), Rome chose the Son, the image of total submission — a terrible mistake. For what does he symbolize? Powerless, tormented, his outstretched arms nailed down so that he cannot take the suffering to his heart, nor raise his fist in wrath against the persecutors and despoilers. Resignation has been declared sacred. What are the results? That the left hand does not know what the right hand is doing. That the sword will be raised against those who most deserve solicitude and consolation. That for many years to come, the earth will be scorched, life despised, humanity trampled into bloody rags. That men will tolerate torture, slavery and starvation. Who will dare to impose another conception of the Son so that we will not be ruined by the omnipotence of the authorities whose criteria are unworldly and supernatural?

Where will the meaning of life be found, if not in the so-called temporal world, in the existence on earth of man, that creature gifted with reason? I do not believe in miracles, nor in the resurrection of the dead, let alone in ascension to the heavens. But I know that militant and at the same time humble consideration for the living, a thirst for justice, can be embodied in a man among men. Only he who loves and understands his fellow men in their affliction and their ignorance, who knows that in a world governed by greed and violence, true compassion requires an iron will and self-discipline — only he who devotes himself in word and deed to making sense of the absurdity, the injustice of being born "fatherless" — that man alone would be an innovator, a giver of life.

Eliezar, you thrust me into the world, first at Alexandria and from there (your experience of men, your mastery of the game of chess taught you to foresee the consequences of certain combinations) to Milan and Rome, to high honor and renown and then finally to humiliation and oblivion, perhaps so that I should learn to be a resistant son, searching for a meaningful place under the sun and not for myself alone. For ten years I taught in the Subura in order to stay alive, because the only trade I could command was language usage and the interpretation of texts.

I had no grandiose expectations for these lessons. I hoped that in the future perhaps some artisans would be able to praise their products in other ways than by the use of clumsy marks, and would know how to compute their expenses and their income, and that a handful of warehousemen and porters might no longer need to stare helplessly at indecipherable characters. It did occur to me, too, that one day these people might be less willing to go on allowing themselves to be treated as doormats and beasts of burden. My ambition and my ability did not reach beyond that.

I know that human nature holds a core of creativity, the germ of individuality. There is a poet, so to speak, in everyone—even Urbanilla, perhaps, half cruel and inquisitive child, half dull and withered flower of the brothel. The true power on earth is the power of poetry. Only the poetic vision, clarifying and connecting, makes life worth living.

If I were able to go on living, I would try to build on what I am only now beginning to understand. Someone — Marcus Anicius Rufus, I suppose — found an opportunity to send me a vial with a few drops of poison — a friendly service from a Roman of the old school, to spare me the humiliation of an execution "in the spirit of the law". But it seems that the powers-that-be have reserved another sort of death for me. I must become — according to him who has unwittingly proved to be your most perfect instrument because for the second time he has been able to provoke me to rebellion — what I have always been, from the very beginning: a prisoner for life. Thanks to this gift, I can, this last time, escape from his control. Voluntary death is also a form of resistance.

Thus a testament and last will. I possess only the will to rise, like the Phoenix, from my earlier self. That impulse I dedicate to you, Eliezar, father. I am one with you and still irrevocably another. You abandoned me; now I leave you forever. I love you and I reject you.

Farewell.

6.

When, later than usual, the Prefect sets foot on the black-and-white marble floor of the justice hall, the sight of his officials, scribes, assessors and attendants arranged in a half-circle before him on the dais, brings home to him the full significance of what he had done that morning. He is not a solitary agent, responsible for his own decisions alone — he represents a structure that begins at the bottom with the praetorian guard and ends at the top with the Emperor himself. If the Prefect errs, he undermines the prestige of the Imperial Majesty; he weakens the widespread apparatus of justice and police power. The argument that he had formulated in the still hours of the night to justify the release ("the sentence pronounced ten years ago must be revoked; the guilt of the accused was not conclusively established") calls into question the whole system of prosecution for divination, most notably by making public the practice — inevitable in this sort of process — of using a network of informers and provocateurs.

The nature of the silence which greets him con-

245

vinces the Prefect that the situation has been discussed before his arrival; the air is filled with repressed tension. He takes his place, pushes his right foot in its red senatorial shoe to the edge of the platform, arranges the folds of his toga. While he is doing this, he realizes that, contrary to custom, he has not asked for nor received the documents for the cases at hand.

The Commandant Aulus Fronto appears at the door, surrounded by his men. This in itself is not unusual: the detachment of the praetorian guard which makes the arrest must be present at every session of the court. However this time the Commandant does not move to the side of the hall, but stands in the middle, before the dais, on the meandering mosaic. He requests permission to speak.

"In the cell of the released prisoner, a small sealed vial was discovered, which, after inquiry, was found to contain a quick-acting poison. This vial was not on the person of the prisoner when he was locked up yesterday afternoon. It follows therefore that it must have been delivered to him later, in secret. I, Aulus Fronto, Commandant of the third division, praetorian guard, consider it my duty to report this fact, since I am responsible for irregularities in the prison vaults."

One of the guard now hands a small bottle of opaque glass to the Prefect, who lifts it unthinking to his face, smells the odor of bitter almonds. Absently, he lets the fragile shell glide back and forth between his fingers, while the Commandant continues.

"This morning about sunrise, on written order of the illustrious Hadrian, Prefect of the City, I had the doors of the prison opened in order to effect the release of the man who called himself Niliacus. It lies within the power of the Prefect to discharge from further prosecution because of lack of evidence, this man, who was encountered on the grounds of the villa of Marcus Anicius Rufus, and interrogated in connection with that arrest. However, this person who called himself Niliacus, is none other than Claudius Claudianus, poet, who was, at an earlier time, condemned to exclusion from fire and water, but who has since returned inside the territory of the City, an act forbidden to him on pain of death. Therefore in this case the Prefect is required to execute the customary sentence.

"I, Aulus Fronto, Commandant of the third

division of the praetorian guard, am not in a position to refuse to implement the commands of my superiors in rank. But I cannot contribute, through my obedience, to this violation and evasion of the law. Therefore I request to be relieved of my duties."

Now the Prefect, as highest magistrate of the City, is still sitting on his ivory throne. On either side of him the *lictors* raise the bundled rods and axes, the *fasces*, symbol of his rank. But he is already no more than a pile of ashes; a breath of wind will suffice to blow him away, and he knows it.

The stirring and whispering behind him has an unmistakably hostile character; short taps with his signet ring will never again call this company to order. The face of the Commandant Aulus Fronto, exemplary soldier, betrays no emotion, but his bearing is grimly inflexible. He stands there, legs apart, chin raised, a personification of the principles strictly upheld for years by the Prefect himself; a perfect product of the Prefect's beliefs and behavior, spirit of his spirit, a relentless supporter of his doctrine, a representative of the new generation of order and discipline, the true son.

The Prefect is surprised: he had always known that

he was not loved; he had never realized how much he was disliked.

He recognizes this feeling of desperation. He is standing with his back against the basalt; there is no escape. From outside, over the buildings of the former temple of Tellus, through the small high windows of the justice hall, come the sounds of Rome, like the murmur of the sea, the rustle of waves rolling over myriad pebbles on the ocean floor.

It takes a simple gesture: to raise the thin glass vial to his lips. An odor of bitter almonds.

GLOSSARY

Arians: Followers of Arius who believed that the Son is not co-equal with the Father.

Atrium: The fore-court, that part of the Roman house opening off the entrance.

Clarissimi: Excellencies.

Clarissimus: Title given in the Imperial period to people of quality.

Clivus Capitolinus: The road to the Capitol.

Curiales: Members of the Curia or court, which was one of the 30 parts into which Romulus divided the Roman people.

Divinatio: divination.

Fasces: A bundle carried before the highest magistrates and consisting of rods, with which criminals were scourged, and an axe with which they were beheaded.

Garum: A sauce for fish.

Gigantomachia: The war between the gods and the Titans.

Homo novus: A man newly ennobled, the first of his family to achieve the highest rank. Sometimes, an upstart.

Ignotus: unknown.

Illustrissimi: Those who are most illustrious.

Impluvium: A skylight, the opening in the roof of the atrium through which smoke was released. It also admitted the rain, and the *impluvium* was also the name for the square basin into which rain water was received.

Insula: A tenement, housing for the poor.

Lares: Protective deities of a house: household gods whose images stood on the hearth in a little shrine.

Libanios: A celebrated 4th century rhetorician (314-393).

Liber pater: The Italian god of fertility. He was commonly identified with the Greek god

Dionysus, although Liber does not seem to have any connection with wine. Romans connected his name with *libertas*: liberty.

Lictor: An attendant granted to a Roman magistrate as a sign of official dignity. The *lictor* bore the *fasces*, the bundle of rods with a protruding axe.

Ludi magister: Schoolmaster.

Magister militum: Supreme Head of the Army.

Magister officiorum: Chief of Chancellery.

Magna Mater: The Great Goddess, Cybele. She was a mother goddess, primarily a goddess of fertility, but also a goddess of wild nature. The cult of the Great Goddess was one of the important mystery religions of the Roman Empire. Her temple was on the Palatine Hill.

Nobilissimi: The Imperial nobility.

Oratorium: A place of prayer, an oratory.

Palla: A long, wide upper garment worn by Roman women. A robe or mantle.

Pater familias: The male head of the family.

Penates: Old Latin guardian deities of the household.

Peristylium: A peristyle, an open space, as a courtyard, surrounded by columns.

Pietas: Dutiful conduct toward the gods and one's family.

Praefectus Praetorio Orientis: Governor of the Eastern Empire.

Progymnasmata: Rhetorical exercises.

Pro Se: Himself; in one's own behalf.

Popina: A tavern.

Sacrificium: Sacrifice.

Stola: A long robe.

Tablinum: A gallery, a room separating the peristyle from the atrium.

Tepidarium: A tepid bathing room.

Triclinium: A dining room, and also a couch running around 3 sides of a table, a table-couch, on which to recline at meals.

Tullianum: The dungeon of the state prison in

Rome, built by King Servius Tullius.

Twelve Tables: The earliest Roman code of laws drawn up by a special commission of ten in 451 B.C. on the demand of the plebians. It is known only from quotations and references; no complete text survives. The Tables dealt with all aspects of the law and gradually became obsolete, as new laws were enacted.

Vigiles: Watchmen.

Volumen: Book roll or scroll.